The

Long-los

When billionaire Mark Hinton is declared dead,
a search begins for his three long-lost children.
These heirs must be found as soon as possible
and flown to New York to claim their rightful
inheritance.

Their new wealth will change their lives forever, but
what these three siblings aren't expecting is to find
the one thing money can't buy...love!

Meet the first heir, Leni, in

Cinderella's Billion-Dollar Christmas

Available now!

And discover the other two heirs in 2020!

Dear Readers,

This book was one of the most difficult books for me to write but also one of the stories I'm the most proud of. Nick's journey of loss doesn't mirror my own experience after the loss of my son, but there are touch points. Overlaps. Grief is hard. Grief is a journey.

One of the most poignant aspects is when you realize you are moving on and something inside you rebels at that. You seem to lose your loved one a second time when you realize you aren't thinking of them as much as you used to.

But life goes on. And Nick desperately needs the sass and warmth Leni brings to his life. He just isn't sure he can accept it.

Luckily, Leni is a fighter. And perfect for Nick. Their story unfolds in bursts of laughter and bouts of sadness...but always at the core is that wonderful experience of falling into something so magnificent you lose your breath and can't help taking the next step.

As odd as it may sound, this book will make you laugh more than it makes you cry as you experience the wonder of finding real love where it's least expected.

Enjoy.

Susan Meier

Cinderella's Billion-Dollar Christmas

Susan Meier

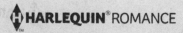

Recycling programs
for this product may
not exist in your area.

ISBN-13: 978-1-335-49963-9

Cinderella's Billion-Dollar Christmas

First North American publication 2019

Copyright © 2019 by Linda Susan Meier

This edition published by arrangement with Harlequin Books S.A.

For questions and comments about the quality of this book, please contact us at CustomerService@Harlequin.com.

Printed in U.S.A.

Susan Meier is the author of over fifty books for Harlequin. *The Tycoon's Secret Daughter* was a Romance Writers of America RITA® Award finalist, and *Nanny for the Millionaire's Twins* won the Book Buyers Best Award and was a finalist in the National Readers' Choice Awards. Susan is married and has three children. One of eleven children herself, she loves to write about the complexity of families and totally believes in the power of love.

Books by Susan Meier

Harlequin Romance

Manhattan Babies

Carrying the Billionaire's Baby
A Diamond for the Single Mom
Falling for the Pregnant Heiress

The Princes of Xaviera

Pregnant with a Royal Baby!
Wedded for His Royal Duty

The Vineyards of Calanetti

A Bride for the Italian Boss

Daring to Trust the Boss
The Twelve Dates of Christmas
Her Brooding Italian Boss
A Mistletoe Kiss with the Boss
The Boss's Fake Fiancée
The Spanish Millionaire's Runaway Bride

Visit the Author Profile page
at Harlequin.com for more titles.

For Mikie. I still miss you every day.

Praise for
Susan Meier

"Meier sucked me into this remarkable love story from the first page and I could not put it down...a captivating love story."

—*Goodreads* on *A Mistletoe Kiss with the Boss*

CHAPTER ONE

LENI LONG STARED out the big front window of the Family Diner in Mannington, Kansas, watching snow cover the sparkly gold Christmas bells hanging from the town's eight streetlights. With the breakfast rush over and the red-and-white-themed diner empty, a hush had fallen over the tiny town.

A black SUV pulled into a parking space a few feet down from the diner. A tall man in a charcoal-gray overcoat exited. His broad shoulders hunched against the snow-laced wind, but there was a strength, a power to the movement. Maybe because of his size. He had to be over six feet and was built like someone who'd spent time in the military. Snow dotted dark hair that had been cut in a sleek, sexy way that sharpened the angles of his handsome face.

A thrill ran through her. Mannington didn't have any men that gorgeous, that male, and he was heading toward the diner.

She raced behind the counter as his long strides

ate up the sidewalk between his SUV and the door. It opened. He stepped inside, turning to close it behind him before he faced her.

His gaze cruised from her candy-cane-print blouse, red apron, short green skirt and red tights to her black patent leather buckle shoes.

Damn it! The first fabulous-looking man to come to Mannington in decades and she was wearing an elf suit.

Oh, well. That was life in a small town. Waitresses dressed like elves. The cook sat outside on the back steps smoking. And her mom, the second waitress for the breakfast shift that morning, hadn't thought twice about calling to say she wouldn't be in until after ten. This was one of those mornings she needed to stay with Leni's dad, making sure he was okay because his head injury from a work accident was now causing small seizures.

Gorgeous Guy peered at the name tag on her blouse. "Leni?"

It wasn't unusual for an out-of-town customer to read her name tag and call her Leni to be friendly, but something about the way he'd said it hit her funny. As if he were disappointed.

"Yes." She smiled. "That's my name."

He ambled over to the counter. "You're the only waitress here?"

She grabbed a nearby cloth and ran it along the

worn white countertop. "Yes. The other waitress is coming in later."

"How much later?"

That was a stupid question. Why would he care what time her mom came in? "She'll be here any minute now." She laughed. "But really, it's fine. I can take your order."

"Okay." He sat on one of the round red stools at the counter. "I'll have a cup of coffee."

"Sure." She turned to the pot sitting on a two-burner warmer behind her. "And you should know that it might be after ten, but the cook makes breakfast all day."

"Sorry. I had breakfast."

Drat. That was her only angle to keep him here. Now he'd drink his cup of coffee and race off—

She frowned. Unless he planned to wait for her mom?

Fears about insurance adjusters and private investigators sent by At Home Construction to spy on her dad raced through her. After two years, the company was arguing his workers' comp and questioning medical bills because they believed he could perform light-duty tasks and come back on the job.

But if this guy wanted to catch her dad working around the house to prove he was no longer disabled, he wouldn't come looking for her mother.

Would he?

No. He'd spy on her dad.

Feeling guilty for thinking the handsome stranger was a private detective, she swiped the cloth down the counter again. "Maybe you'd like a cinnamon roll?"

He laughed. "No. Thank you."

His words were kind, but precise. Leni smiled. He didn't need food and sometimes customers didn't want to talk. She would leave to him to his coffee.

She turned to walk away, but he said, "Nice town you have here."

She faced him again. "Mannington's okay."

His dark brows rose. "Only okay?"

Maybe he did want to talk? And maybe a few minutes of personal time with him would stop her from being suspicious? His brown eyes lit with a hint of amusement and this close he was so gorgeous it was fun just looking at him.

No harm in enjoying that.

"No. Mannington's a great place, but I'll be moving soon. I just finished my degree and I'm probably going to have to relocate to Topeka to get a job." She shrugged. "That's the way it is sometimes. If you want to work, you go to the big city."

"I'm from New York. My family owns a money management firm. I always knew where I'd be employed. Went through a bit of a rebellious phase, but I think everybody does, and here I am."

In Mannington, Kansas?

A guy who owned a New York City money management firm was in Mannington, Kansas, where no one had any money?

Her suspicions rose again. But at least they were talking. Maybe with a little good old-fashioned waitress chitchat she could get him to tell her why he was here?

Especially if he was looking for her mom.

Nick Kourakis couldn't stop staring at the woman behind the counter. He'd been sent by the estate of Mark Hinton to find Elenore Long, probably the waitress who hadn't yet arrived, and instead he'd run into the most naturally beautiful woman he'd ever seen.

She had an exquisite face, a perfect figure that her goofy elf suit couldn't hide and big green eyes that shone with humor—

Until he'd asked when the other waitress would be coming in. Then she'd gotten quiet. But now that they were talking about her getting a job, things had perked up again. It didn't matter what he told her or what she told him. They'd never see each other again. That was the beauty of a conversation with a stranger. It was pointless. Exactly the diversion he needed while he waited for Elenore Long.

"So, you think you'll be moving to Topeka?"

She shrugged. "Probably."

He gestured at the candy-cane blouse. "Gonna take the elf suit?"

She laughed. "I doubt they let social workers wear them."

He loved her laugh. He loved her flowing hair. He loved that a little small talk had brought back her smile. "That's a tough job."

"I know."

"But it should be fairly easy to find work."

Her smile grew into a grin. "I know that, too."

"Well, there's just no fooling you, is there, Leni?"

She smiled again. Her full lips lifting and her green eyes sparkling.

He swore to God his heart turned over in his chest. He'd been single for so long that he couldn't remember the last time he'd had this kind of reaction to a woman. Not just an instant connection, but a welcome connection, as if the small talk he thought so pointless was a door to something—

Looking at her beautiful face, big eyes, high cheekbones, perfect nose, and lips just made for kissing, he almost suggested she search for work in New York, but that would be as pointless as a conversation about the weather. Why would he ask a beautiful woman to make such a drastic move for him, when he knew nothing would come of it?

The diner door opened and he turned. A woman in an elf suit just like Leni's walked in.

The other waitress. Most likely Elenore Long.

His eyes narrowed as he studied her. She was fifty, at least. Her chestnut hair curled around a square face and her eyes were blue. His heiress was the first of three children fathered by Mark Hinton, who'd died two weeks ago at the age of sixty. This woman was too old to be his child, even his firstborn.

He rose from his stool. "*You're* the other waitress?"

The woman began unbuttoning her coat. "Yeah."

"I think he's been waiting for you, Mom."

Nick swung to face Leni again. "Mom?"

"That's my mom. Denise Long, Mr. Owner-of-a-Money-Management-Firm. If you think we got a settlement to invest after my dad's injury, you're wrong. We can barely get the insurance company to pay his medical bills."

He fell to the round red stool again. "I'm not after your dad's money." He took a quick breath and caught Leni's gaze. "Your last name is Long?"

"Yeah."

Not taking any chances, he said, "And Leni is a nickname for something?"

He waited for confirmation but deep down he already knew the answer.

"Elenore."

He ran his fingers along his brow. "Elenore Long." He shook his head. If he hadn't been so blinded by her bedroom eyes, glorious mane of hair and sexy little body, he probably would have figured that out. "You're Elenore Long?"

She nodded. "Yes."

"Is there someplace private you and I can talk?"

She pressed her hand to her chest. "*I'm* the person you're here to see?"

"Yes."

"Why? I could barely get student loans. I don't have anything to hand over to a money management firm."

"Seriously. We have to talk someplace private." He caught her gaze. "Now."

Leni had never seen anybody's mood shift so quickly. He went from cute and flirty to serious in under a second. But that was fine since she was totally confused by him. First, he wanted to talk to her mom. Now he wanted to talk to her?

"The only people in the diner are you, me and my mom. George, the cook, is outside smoking." She glanced around. "We can just go to one of the booths in the back."

"Okay." He pointed to the last booth in the farthest corner. "We'll sit there."

He walked behind her until they reached the table. Then he slid onto the bench across from her.

"My name is Nick Kourakis. I work for a money management firm in New York City."

"So, you said. And I told you my family doesn't have any money to invest."

"I know."

His eyes darkened as he studied her. With all his attention centered on her face, she had to hold back a shudder. She had never seen a man this good-looking. But as she thought that, she noticed that his gray overcoat was stunningly made, and his white shirt and tie looked expensive. As big as he was, he wore both effortlessly, as if he was accustomed to luxury. Maybe even made for it.

She suddenly realized he wasn't gorgeous so much as he was a combination of the whole package. Expensive clothes. Sparkling clean. Handsome.

And wealthy.

Probably so rich, she couldn't even fathom the amount of money he had.

"I'm not selling anything. I'm not even here on behalf of the money management firm. I was sent here to retrieve you."

"Retrieve me?" His sultry brown eyes held her captive, sending warmth swimming through her blood, confusing her, almost hypnotizing her.

"Because I have some exciting news for you."

"Oh, yeah?" She fought the strange sensations assaulting her with sarcasm. "And what would that be?"

"First, what I have to tell you *has to* remain confidential."

Some of her equilibrium returned. "Okay."

He leaned back on the bench. "Have you ever heard of Mark Hinton?"

More of her confidence came back. Enough to put starch in her spine. "No."

"He's a billionaire…or was. We have reason to believe you are one of the people mentioned in his will."

"Oh…" Her composure took a tumble. Imagining herself getting as much as ten thousand dollars and paying off some of the bills that had accumulated since her dad's injury, she told her wishful-thinking brain to stop before she got her hopes up. "That's good. Right?"

"It could potentially be wonderful."

"Dude, wonderful to me is enough money to pay my dad's medical bills."

"It's more than that."

New thoughts scrambled around in her brain. Like buying her dad the service dog he needed because of his seizures, and not worrying about the company forcing him back to work.

But as quickly as her good thoughts set up shop, some bad thoughts came tumbling in. Adopted at eight, after a year in foster care when her biological mom gave her up, she'd always believed she was not a lucky person. The way she'd struggled for eight years just to afford her basic bachelor's degree backed that up. "What's the catch?"

"Before I say another word, I need your promise that you won't talk about this with anyone until I tell you that you can."

A laugh bubbled out. "You want me to take a vow of silence?"

"You are the first of three potential heirs to Mark Hinton's estate. A *huge* estate. You can tell your parents, but that's it. And they have to promise to keep this news to themselves. Frankly, it's a matter of *your* personal safety."

It all seemed to so preposterous that it couldn't sink in. As good as it would be to be rich, she was much too practical to believe in magic or miracles. It had to be a joke or a mistake.

When she said nothing, he sighed. "Do you have your phone?"

She pulled it out of her apron pocket.

"Search *Mark Hinton*."

She did as he said, though she mumbled, "Anybody can put up a fake website."

But her phone produced eight thousand results for Mark Hinton. Her gaze leaped to Nick's. "What is this?"

"Information on his life." He paused for a second before he added, "I was sent here by the law firm handling your dad's estate. The attorney in charge is stuck in court today. He's a friend of mine, and my family's firm manages your father's fortune, so I was picked to come in his place."

She barely heard anything after he said "your dad's estate." Her breath stumbled. "My *dad's*?"

She struggled to take it all in. Her biological mom hadn't told her anything about her father. She would always say he wasn't important, and they didn't need him. At seven, she'd known that wasn't true when her mom couldn't afford to keep her anymore.

"According to the estate lawyer, the paper trail says Mark Hinton is your father," Nick said. "But they'll be getting DNA."

She leaned back in disappointment and disbelief, her voice dull when she said, "My biological father was rich."

"One of the first multibillionaires." Nick shifted. "If you let this get out before the estate has a chance to protect you, you will be mobbed by people who want money. You'll be a target for scam artists and kidnappers. I came here not merely to tell you, but to take you to New York so the lawyer can make the process of vetting you easier for *you*."

Something Leni couldn't define or describe fluttered through her, tightening her chest, making her head spin. She looked at the eight *thousand* results to her search and saw the words *billionaire, reclusive, oil and gas prodigy* and *missing heirs*.

Her heart stopped then burst to life again with such a frantic beat she thought she'd faint. This would be more than enough money to care for her dad.

"You think this guy is my father and I'm one of these heirs?"

"The estate lawyer is fairly certain you're one of the heirs. He says the paper trail is solid. But they'll do a DNA test to confirm it."

Her voice came out as a squeak as she said, "Okay."

"For confidentiality purposes and for your safety, you have to go to New York now." He paused long enough to catch her gaze. "Will you come with me?"

Ten minutes ago, that offer probably would have scrambled her pulse. Now? The happy, flirty guy was gone. A businessman had replaced him.

She almost missed the flirty guy. But her brain had been captured by the idea that she might be wealthy enough that her parents would no longer have to worry about money.

Still, she wasn't going to New York with a man she didn't know, based solely on his word. "Give me a day?"

"The plan was to leave as soon as we told you."

She shook her head. "I want a day. Twenty-four hours to explain all this to my parents and to check you out."

"I can provide you with references—"

"No thanks. I'll find what I need on my own." She'd check every dark and moldy corner of the internet if she had to, to make sure he was for real.

There was no way she'd leave for New York with a stranger. And no way she'd get her parents' hopes up for nothing.

CHAPTER TWO

NICK KOURAKIS LEFT the diner, a mix of disappointment and confusion slowing his steps. He should have been focused on the fact that this unexpected trip was a chance to convince Leni Long to keep her dad's money with his money management firm. But Danny Manelli, attorney for the estate, didn't want him making a pitch to her. A clause in the will could give the estate trouble, and Nick could make it worse by talking about money before Danny could properly explain the clause to Leni.

Now that he had given her the basics that would get her to New York to start the process of vetting her, Nick wasn't supposed to talk about anything except the weather and football. Two things Danny was sure wouldn't accidentally tip them into talking about the estate.

That was good, sound logic. And normally Nick would be totally onboard with it. Instead, he was gobsmacked. Leni Long was the first woman he'd been overwhelmingly attracted to in a decade. But it was more than that. Something about her clicked with him. And that was so odd he couldn't shake the feeling.

Telling himself that was absurd, he walked down the sidewalk and jumped into the passenger seat of the SUV.

Behind the steering wheel, Jace MacDonald, owner of Around the World Security, said, "Where's the girl?"

"She wants a day to investigate us."

Jace shook his head, then shifted to face Nick, the gun beneath his black leather jacket visible when he turned. "It's going to be difficult to keep an eye on her here. Even for twenty-four hours." He motioned outside. "Not only are the houses and businesses spaced in such a way that an extra person sticks out like a sore thumb, but so do cars. You should have seen the people sniffing around the SUV while you were in the diner. A strange vehicle parked on a street where everybody knows everybody else's car? That's like a neon sign."

"I don't care. You heard what Danny said. That woman is worth more money than the gross national products of several small countries combined. If the wrong people find out, she'll be a target."

"Yeah, of banks that want to compete for her business." Jace snickered. "You do realize Danny's keeping you from an excellent opportunity to convince her to keep her share of the estate with you?"

Nick peeked at him. "You're not allowed to pitch your company either."

Jace raised his hands in disgust. "Got the same sermon you did."

"Then you know the problem with the will. After a few charitable bequests, Mark divides the remainder of his estate between his first child and any subsequent heirs. A good lawyer could argue that that gives Mark's first child half, with the other half split between the other two kids. Danny wants to be the one to explain it to Elenore."

Jace sniffed. "How the hell can pitching our companies' services affect that stupid clause?"

"He just wants to be sure we don't accidentally say something we shouldn't."

"That's ridiculous." Jace growled.

Nick totally understood his frustration, but he didn't want to do anything that could make trouble for Danny. "Look, you knew Mark. He was a good guy. Nine chances out of ten, he wanted that estate distributed equally among his heirs. I'm sure Danny has a plan to get all three of Mark's kids on board with that. That's why he doesn't want us talking to her. Muddying the waters."

"Right." Jace pulled the gear shift out of Park and headed toward the interstate. "There isn't a hotel or even a bed and breakfast in this town. I'll drive you up the highway until we find one, then I have to get back here to figure out a way to hide myself and this boat of an SUV we rented so I can watch her tonight."

Nick winced. "Sorry. I couldn't talk her into leaving today."

"Not to worry. I'll deal with it. How are you going to handle the fact that she wanted time to check *you* out?" He laughed. "What's she going to find when she does a search on you?"

Nick faced the window. "Nothing."

"You're sure? The guy they call the New Wolf of Wall Street doesn't have a skeleton?"

Nick said, "No skeleton," but he lied. He'd talked his only brother into going out on a night when the roads were icy. A former Navy SEAL, he counted on himself to be one of the best drivers in unusual situations. But a combination of icy roads and other cars had bested him that night, and his only sibling had been killed.

But that was five years ago, and he didn't think the story even popped up in internet searches anymore.

"Come on. Nobody meets a guy like Hinton without a story."

"I did."

That part was true. He'd met Mark Hinton in Dubai. They'd gambled. They'd skydived. They'd talked money. Especially investment strategy. In Nick's world, there was nothing special about any of that. After Mark decided to trust Kourakis

Money Management with most of his fortune, they'd had meetings on his yachts or while fishing in the Florida Keys. They drank tequila, talked about his financial goals and even about the kids who were now Mark's heirs. Though never while Mark was sober. Powerful men didn't admit weakness or failures without a nudge. Mark's nudge was alcohol. With enough tequila, Mark would talk about his kids—without mentioning their names—and Nick would nurse his regret and sorrow over his brother's death. *That* was why Mark was comfortable with Nick. Even with a thirty-year age difference, they understood each other. Understood mistakes. Understood regret.

Even now, it trickled from his subconscious to the front of his brain. He'd been too confident, cocky even. His brother hadn't wanted to go out that night. His parents hadn't wanted them to go. But he'd been so sure—

He was always so sure.

After Joe's death, he'd had to stop jet-setting, return to New York and take over the family business.

But he was still the same guy deep down inside. Instead of taking risks on the slopes or in the sky, he played with money.

And no one beat him.

Ever.

He'd gotten so good at what he did that he liked it. Until he recalled the reason why he was the

"New Wolf." Even now, the grief of losing his brother sent guilt oozing through him.

He didn't understand what had happened to him in that diner that he'd forgotten Joe, forgotten his guilt and laughed with someone he barely knew. But when they returned to New York, he'd be focused again, diligent. If he was going to lose even part of the Hinton money when the estate was settled and one or two of the heirs decided to hire new money management, he'd have to find big investors to replace it.

He would not let his parents down twice.

Leni's mom only worked until two o'clock, but Leni's shift didn't end until three. Having evaded her questions about Nick Kourakis, taking Nick's warnings seriously about the complications of people finding out she might be an heiress, Leni raced home and found her parents in the kitchen.

"Hey."

Sitting at the center island, her dad looked up from his newspaper.

Her mom glanced over from the stove. "Hey. Finally going to tell us what the guy in the overcoat wanted?"

Leni forced a smile. Denise and Jake Long had adopted her when she was in the gangly stage for a little girl. No longer an adorable infant or cute toddler, with a bit of a history of being difficult at school, most potential parents overlooked her.

The Longs had given her a home, made her their daughter. Now she didn't merely know she had a biological mom out there somewhere who had given her up; she might have had a rich dad who hadn't wanted her at all.

Once again, she thanked God for her adoptive parents.

She took a seat beside her dad. "First, what I'm about to say is a secret. So, you can't tell anybody."

Her mom said, "Okay," as her dad nodded.

"The guy in the overcoat was Nick Kourakis. He owns a management firm in New York, and he told me that I might have inherited some money."

Her dad's weathered face brightened. A lifelong construction worker, he had wrinkles around his eyes that appeared when he smiled. "Well, that's great!"

Her mother gasped and walked over from the stove to hug Leni. "I'm so happy for you."

"Yeah, well, it's not assured. I have to go to New York. There will also be a DNA test to confirm my identity. Honestly, I won't quite believe all this is true until DNA says I'm an heir. So, our not mentioning this to anybody protects me from embarrassing myself if it doesn't pan out."

Part of her almost wished it wouldn't. If her biological father had been a struggling factory worker, she could have understood him not being able to take responsibility for her, but a guy who was rich and not paying child support, forcing her mom to give her up when she got sick? When it was a decision between the medicine she needed and feeding her child?

It was demeaning, insulting, infuriating.

She'd have to deal with that if Mark Hinton really was her biological father. Those feelings would all go away if he wasn't.

Her dad leaned back in his chair. "It's always good not to get your hopes up, Kitten. But maybe this family's due for some good luck?"

And that was the catch. Part of her would like to tell Nick Kourakis to take her biological dad's money and shove it. She was educated now. She had a career path. She would be fine.

But her parents wouldn't.

They'd never ask her for a dime, but she wouldn't make them ask. If she'd inherited enough money to care for her dad, she wanted it.

"Okay." She slid off her chair. "I'm going upstairs to do some investigating into everything. I'm not getting on a plane with a guy I don't know."

Her dad smiled. "That's smart, my girl."

The simple comment hit her right in the heart. She was his girl. *His* girl. Not the child of some sperm donor who'd never even checked to see if she was okay.

That was not a father.

* * *

Almost twenty-four hours from when Leni had met him, Nick Kourakis and a man she didn't recognize pulled into the driveway of the Long residence in the big, black SUV. Nick had looked up her parents' home phone number and called her the night before to say they'd be leaving at ten o'clock. He'd given her time to research him and his firm, to talk to her parents and to pack for a couple weeks in Manhattan, but that was it. They needed to get her safely to New York.

Her breath frosty in the cold, last-day-of-November air, she hugged and kissed her short, curly-haired mom and balding dad, saying goodbye at the front door of their house, her conflicted feelings about Mark Hinton dogging her.

Nick handed Danny Manelli's business card to her parents, telling them that he was the lawyer in charge of the estate and if they had any questions, they could call him. Then he introduced her to Jace MacDonald, the guy in the black leather jacket who directed her to the back seat of the SUV. Nick got in beside her.

She frowned at the empty passenger's seat in the front.

"Jace owns Around the World Security. He'll be your bodyguard while you're in New York."

She gaped at Nick. "Bodyguard?"

Jace caught her gaze in the rearview mirror.

"Trust me. If you're worth billions, you'll need one."

She huffed out a breath. "Billions?"

Nick laughed. "Yes. Mark Hinton had billions. With an *s*. Plural. As in many billions."

"I know. I researched him last night, too. It's just so hard to believe."

She shook her head and looked out the window. The guy had billions and he had left her mom so broke she'd had to put Leni into foster care.

The insult of it stiffened her spine.

Jace made a few turns and they headed north. Twenty minutes later, he pulled the SUV onto a private airstrip. When they drove up to a sleek red and silver jet, she gasped. "Holy cow."

Nick laughed. "That plane is nothing. I'm just a simple billionaire."

She knew that, too. She'd spent forty minutes the night before reading about how successful the investment arm of his family's money management firm was. What she hadn't expected was that they'd be riding in *his* plane. Not when her biological father was supposed to have so much money.

Something about that just seemed off.

She faced Nick again. "This plane is yours?"

"Yes."

He glanced over, catching her gaze, and her breath shivered.

Damn it. Now was not the time to be feeling

that stupid attraction she had to him. Not only did he seem to be in charge of her, but she was too confused about her potential biological dad to add an attraction into the mix. Plus, there was something wrong with Nick using his own plane to get her. This was not the man to be attracted to.

Jace exited the SUV and came around to her door to open it. She climbed out at the same time Nick did.

Nick led her to the small stack of stairs and into the jet. She had to hold back a gasp when she stepped inside. Three small groupings of white leather seats were arranged around the large cabin. The little windows had elegant gray shades. A silver and black bar sat discreetly in a back corner. A rich red carpet covered the floor.

She took a slow, measured breath. She could not be a country bumpkin about this. She had to stay sharp.

Pretending a calm she didn't feel, she stopped by the first group of seats and slid out of her worn leather jacket.

Behind her, Nick said, "The flight's about three hours. Then, because we use an airstrip outside the city, we'll have about an hour-and-a-half limo ride."

"Limo ride?" She swallowed, picturing her blue-collar self, in her ancient leather jacket and worn jeans, getting into a limo.

He took her coat and handed it to the flight attendant who scurried to the back of the jet with it.

"Don't worry. You'll acclimate. After a day or two in New York, you'll realize a limo's the easiest way to get around the city. Just like this jet is the most comfortable way to get from place to place."

He motioned to the rear of the cabin. "The first room you walk into back there is a kitchen. If you want a snack you just ask Marie, but she'll be serving lunch at noon. So, a snack might not be a good idea. Beyond that is an office-slash-den, complete with a pullout bed. Jace will probably go back there once we take off." He winced. "He stayed up most of the night keeping an eye on your house. He'll need the nap."

"He stayed up all night?"

"That's his job, remember?"

She did. She simply hadn't connected him being a bodyguard to him sitting in his SUV all night watching her house.

"You'll get used to it. For now, settle in. Get accustomed to the convenience that's your new lifestyle."

She couldn't fathom riding in a limo let alone owning a jet. "If I'm an heir."

"The lawyer for the estate all but said your DNA test is only a formality." He pointed to the rear of the plane. "I have some work to do, so I'll be back there if there's anything you need."

He turned to leave but she said, "Why are we in your jet instead of one of my dad's?"

Nick faced her again. "What?"

"Why are we using your jet instead of one of Mark Hinton's?"

"We're not using one of Mark's jets because we're not using anything belonging to Hinton Holdings."

"Why?"

He sighed. "We don't want to alert anyone that we might have found an heir before we confirm you."

"Because?"

This time he pulled in a long breath, obviously losing patience with her questions. "This estate is worth so much money that everyone in the world is curious about who you are. Danny devised a plan to find the heirs and keep you safe. Not using estate property is part of it. If we start using jets or houses and cars, people will know something is up and begin snooping. The longer we can keep the press and curiosity seekers at bay, the better."

She held the gaze of his dark eyes for a second, then she shook her head. She didn't think he was lying. But she did know he hadn't told her everything. Until her DNA results were back, she probably didn't have the right to push him. But she would watch him, pay attention to every word he said, because there was definitely something going on with him.

* * *

Nick breathed a sigh of relief as he headed to the seat in the back of the plane. He didn't mind her questions. They were generic enough that he could answer them. It was her nearness that threw him for a loop. He was smarter than this, more in control. His whole body shouldn't buzz just because they were standing close.

He reached the plush leather seat, but before he sat, he realized he'd forgotten his briefcase. He returned to the front and opened the overhead bin above the seat Leni had chosen.

She glanced up at him, her thick lashes blinking over her sultry green eyes, her long brown hair sort of floating around her.

"Forgot my briefcase," he explained, trying not to stumble over his words. "I kept it on the plane, thinking we'd be leaving yesterday."

She smiled in acknowledgment and his heart went from pitter-patter to a drum solo in one breath.

Stifling a groan, he headed to the rear of the cabin again, eager to return to New York to lose these crazy feelings he had around her. Part of it had to be surprise over how pretty she was. Mark Hinton wasn't even a five on a scale of one to ten, but apparently Leni's mother had been a twelve.

The other part was just plain attraction. Serious lust. Something biological that sprang up before he could control it.

So, it was wrong.
Had to be.

He didn't get out-of-control feelings and he sure as hell never let emotions rule him.

A movement in the front caught his attention and he peeked up to see Leni get out of her seat to put her purse in the overhead bin. Her head fell back as she reached up, sending all that thick, shiny hair bouncing.

This time he allowed himself an internal groan.

This was crazy.

For the first time since Danny had laid down the rules for Nick's trip to retrieve Leni, he was glad he'd been ordered to keep his distance from her. Because whatever he was feeling, he didn't want it. He had priorities, a company to run, parents to keep happy. He couldn't afford the weakness of a hellishly strong attraction.

He put his head down and went to work and didn't look up until hours later when the jet began to descend. Choosing not to go up to the overhead bin again, he secured his briefcase under his seat, fastened his seat belt and waited for the jet to slide onto the ground, relieved that he only had a little over an hour more in her company. He would leave her with Danny and never look back.

CHAPTER THREE

GIVEN THE TIME difference between Kansas and New York, it was almost three o'clock when they landed in New York. Leni had eaten a fabulous lunch, served by Marie, prepared by a chef hiding somewhere in the back. Leni hadn't seen her luggage since climbing into the SUV in Mannington, but she suspected someone had handled it. Nick had said to settle in and get comfortable with luxury...but, come on. A chef who had flown from New York to Mannington and from Mannington back to New York, just to make lunch? On a jet? For her?

It boggled the mind.

They boarded a limo and headed for the city, Leni feeling totally out of place in her worn jacket and jeans. Though Christmas decorations in shop windows, on streetlights and clinging to parking meters gave the area a familiar feel, she had never seen so many buildings in such a small place.

But she didn't mention it. She didn't want to be

attracted to Nick or to mistrust him. But, unfortunately, she felt both things, and mistrust trumped attraction. She wouldn't say anything around him that she didn't have to.

When they pulled up to a building so tall that she couldn't see the top of it, Nick said, "Our first appointment... Your lawyer."

"My lawyer?"

"The lawyer for the estate."

She gasped. "I'm in jeans! You should have told me I'd be meeting him this afternoon. I thought I was only flying here today!"

"You're fine. You're a blue-collar woman who's just been told she might be a billionaire. You don't have to put on airs."

"Lucky thing, since I hadn't given a thought to trying that."

The driver opened the back door. Nick climbed out first and extended his hand to help her exit the limo.

Light snow fell around him, and he pulled her out into it. The shiny white flakes collecting on his dark hair reminded her of seeing him getting out of the SUV and walking to the diner, huddled against the falling snow. All the feelings from the day before came tumbling back. Her attraction. Their small talk. Laughing together.

Close enough to kiss him, she fought the magnetic pull that tried to lure her in, but it was her mistrust that fluttered away. Before she'd known who he was, she'd told Nick about needing to move to Topeka and he'd told her that his family owned a money management firm and he'd had a rebellious streak.

They'd formed a connection and she felt it again, as clearly as if they were still in the diner.

She stepped back, trying to get rid of it and the fears that rushed at her when she realized where she was and why. It didn't work. All her worries tumbled out, even as the sense of connection to Nick held on.

"All I can think about is being embarrassed or scared when it's announced that I'm an heir. Doing something stupid, making a fool of myself—"

He stopped her by putting his hands on her shoulders and looking her in the eye. "You don't have anything to be embarrassed about. And as for being scared, from the couple of hours I've known you, I can tell you're strong. You can do this."

His dark eyes had sharpened with a strength that sent a shot of attraction from her chest to her toes. This was the Nick she'd made a connection with. The nice guy. The guy she'd liked.

She had to swallow before she could say, "Okay."

He took her elbow and directed her toward the building. She swore heat from his touch seeped through her worn leather jacket and to her skin. She didn't know what it was about him that seemed to draw her in, but whatever it was, it was powerful.

A tiny part of her whispered that her feelings were right. That she could trust him. That she *should* trust him.

She really wanted to believe that, especially walking up to a building with so many floors jutting up to the sky she couldn't count them, fancy pillars carved into the exterior walls and a sophisticated medallion resting over the entry like a royal crest.

When they reached the revolving door, her knees wobbled and she was grateful for Nick's hand at her elbow. He released her when they stepped into a lobby with marble floors and red and white poinsettias scattered about. No plastic wreaths. No gaudy ornaments. No blinking lights. Just tasteful flowers. And twenty or thirty people dressed as sophisticatedly as Nick.

Her thoughts scrambled again. He only touched her when she needed help, barely spoke, had ignored her on the plane. He might be the guy from the diner, but he wasn't always nice. He had a job to do—get her to New York—and he was doing it.

She had to stop imagining good things about him.

They walked past a bank of elevators to another row hidden around a corner. These elevators had keypads and Nick had to punch in a series of numbers on the third one for the doors to open.

A man in a power suit came out of the second elevator, followed by a woman in a pencil skirt and silky blouse, visible because her fancy wool coat was unbuttoned. Like people on a mission, they bounded around the corner and off to parts unknown.

She sucked in a long breath, straightened her old jacket and smoothed her hand along the high collar of her turtleneck, hoping it looked newer than it was. Because, man, she was seriously underdressed.

When they stepped out of the elevator into an office, she didn't just think it. She knew it. A wall of glass behind the desk displayed a view of Manhattan that made her breath stutter. The buildings looked close enough to touch. And with so much glass surrounding the room she felt like she was walking on air.

A short, slender woman opened the door on the far left and peeked inside. "Hey, Nick. Could you come into my office for a second?"

Nick glanced at Leni and she forced a smile. "I'm fine. Maybe I'll go over to the window and try to see inside the office across the street."

Nick stifled a laugh, but just barely. Leni had to be the most naturally funny, most open person he'd ever met. He couldn't help comforting her when she'd admitted how afraid she was, but he'd kept his solace short and simple. Because in another ten minutes, he'd be back on that elevator, heading for his own office. His favor for his friend completed. His sanity restored.

He followed Danny's assistant, Mary Catherine, into her office. She pointed at the phone on her desk. "I have Mr. Manelli on the line."

Confusion stopped him where he was. "On the line? He was supposed to be here waiting for us."

She skirted her desk and headed for the hallway. "Why don't you let him explain?"

When she was gone, Nick picked up the receiver of the desk phone and said, "Where the hell are you?"

"Stuck in court. Remember the trial I told you I would be getting a continuance on? The reason I needed you to be the one to retrieve Elenore Long instead of me? Well, the judge didn't go for the continuance. I'm stuck here."

"Stuck there?"

"The judge thinks there's no reason to postpone a trial that won't last more than a few days. It's corporate stuff. Everybody's prepared to the max. It will take a day or two to get through it."

"Why are you telling me this?"

"Because we can't let Elenore Long sit alone in a hotel room this afternoon, tonight and all day tomorrow."

"Danny, I agreed to do this favor for you mostly because Mark was my friend and I knew how he felt about his kids' safety. But that was it."

"That was all I needed when I called you on

Saturday, but through no fault of mine, things changed. That's life. You remember life? If something can go wrong, it usually does."

Understanding that a little better than Danny knew, Nick blew his breath out on a frustrated sigh. "What about Jace? He's the bodyguard. He should be with her. Not me."

"Jace had an emergency come up. He and most of his men are on their way to El Salvador."

He gaped at the phone. "El Salvador!"

"Yep. So, we're down to you. You know all the information about the identity of the heirs and potential heirs has to be kept as quiet as possible. The fewer people who know, the less chance someone will accidentally slip a name to their wife or girlfriend. Besides, you're the most closed-mouthed person I know."

"I'm not a bodyguard!"

"You don't need to be. As long as no one knows who she is, she's just another New York tourist."

"And what the hell do I do with her for the next day…or two?"

Danny's voice lifted with hope. "Anything you want. New York's a big city. As long as you stay away from talking about the estate, you could very easily entertain her for a week."

"A week!"

"Tops. I swear."

Nick squeezed his eyes shut. "You owe me."

"Big time," Danny agreed.

As his friend gave him the name of the hotel he'd booked for Leni, Nick looked through the glass separating Mary Catherine's office and Danny's. Leni stood by the wall of windows staring at the Manhattan skyline, obviously a fish out of water.

And she'd already admitted to being afraid.

He passed his hand down his face. The part of him that wanted to help her was the part he wanted to squelch, destroy, kick so far out of town he wouldn't even think about being attracted to her anymore. He'd planned on doing the eviction tonight with a bottle of scotch and four hours of work. Danny and Jace weren't the only ones with commitments.

Danny sighed. "Look, get her settled in the hotel and take her for a nice dinner."

Nick blew his breath out in exasperation. "I'm serious about this costing you one big, fat favor."

Danny laughed. "Why? Does she look like Mark?"

"No, I'm guessing she got the cocktail waitress's genes."

Danny guffawed. "That good, huh?"

Nick gazed longingly at Leni again. "Better."

"Okay. I've got to go. The judge is back from recess. And I swear I will end this trial as quickly as possible."

As Danny hung up, Nick took a long, slow breath. He didn't want to spend any more time with a woman he was already attracted to. Work was his life now. Besides, she was way too nice for him. Innocent. Sweet. He wasn't any of those. Still, he was helping Danny because Mark had been his friend. He resisted women all the time. This one would be no different.

He walked into Danny's office and straight to the private elevator. "Let's go."

Leni scrambled after him. "Where?"

"The lawyer is stuck in a trial. I'm taking you to your hotel and then to dinner."

They stepped into the elevator. "I can't go to dinner with you."

He peered at her. "You're ditching me?"

"No. I'm just not going out with someone dressed like you," she said, pointing at his black suit and charcoal-gray overcoat. "When I look like this." She motioned down the front of her jacket.

"We can buy you a dress before we go to the hotel. In fact, we can get you anything you want. There's a slush fund for vetting potential heirs. It's there to get you anything you need while you're in the city."

She gaped at him. "I'm not letting you buy me clothes." Though she almost wished she could. Her old jeans and jacket firmly announced her as someone not from Manhattan. Which made her stick out in the crowd milling about in the building lobby. The people who'd seen her walking out of the private elevator for a lawyer's office probably thought she was a petty thief.

"I can't pay you back if I'm not an heir."

"I told you, there's a slush fund. You're in New York at the estate's request. While you're here it's our responsibility to get you anything and everything you need. No paybacks. It's part of the process. We'll be putting the exact same amount of money into slush accounts for all potential heirs."

"You might have to pay for the hotel and the limo, but you're not buying me clothes."

A muscle in his jaw jumped as he motioned to the revolving door. "Fine."

She could see she'd aggravated him, but she didn't care. She walked through the door, out into the snow and into the limo again. They took a short ride and exited the limo onto the busiest street Leni had ever seen. The jumbotron, lights and videos were the familiar backdrop of an early morning news show.

She reverently whispered. "Times Square."

Nick pointed to the right. "Your hotel is this way."

The only hotel she saw to the right was way down the street. She glanced back at the limo. "We're walking?"

"Traffic was backed up at the hotel entry. It's not far."

"Oh. Okay."

"You want to get back into the limo and wait out the line?"

Not really. Cool air massaged her warm face. The noise of Times Square and the crowded street took her attention away from Mark Hinton and money and the handsome guy walking with her who seemed to have gone from annoyed to angry. No sense poking the bear.

"Yeah. Walking's good." Shoving her hands into her jacket pockets, she peered around again. "I like seeing everything."

He pointed across the street. "My office is in that building there."

Gray brick with black slate accents. Long, thin windows. A doorman.

"Wow." She fought the question that automatically rose as she shuffled along beside him, but it bubbled out anyway. "What's it like to work here?" She gestured around her. "In all of this noise and people?"

"Our windows are soundproof."

She laughed. "Seriously? You know what I mean. You saw where I live. There are about fifteen hundred people in our entire town, and I'll bet there are three thousand on this street with us now. You can't know everybody. How do you decide who to trust?"

He peeked at her. "Reputation."

She skipped twice to catch up with his long

strides. "Reputation? If you don't know someone, how do you know their reputation?"

He shrugged. "I always know somebody who knows somebody who knows them. And, if they are high enough in a corporate structure, there will be things written about them."

"Written about them?"

"In professional journals, but I do search the internet sometimes to find out things about them."

"Did you research me?"

He gave her the side-eye. "That was Danny's job."

"This Danny—the lawyer—is pretty important?"

"His firm is handling the Hinton estate. He's the boss. Any mistakes are on him."

Things began to fall in to place for Leni. Nick never lied to her, but she was beginning to understand why getting a complete answer out of him was close to impossible. *She* was the problem.

"Like mistakes you make with me?"

He stopped walking and studied her for a few seconds before he said, "Yes."

That ill-timed thrill ran through her again, and she knew why he'd stopped walking, why he was still looking at her. Their initial conversation at the diner had been flirty and fun and she wasn't a thirteen-year-old girl wondering in the boy next door liked her. She knew the signs. But he'd had to squelch those feelings. Because of the estate? Because of not wanting to make mistakes?

"You aren't allowed to get too chummy with me, are you?"

"No."

"And the reason you keep acting all stuffy is because we sort of already did make friends in the diner?"

"Yes. And that's wrong." He shook his head. "You're funny and you have a warmth about you that's very appealing. But there are things in my life that prevent me from even considering a relationship, and you could potentially be inheriting tons of money which will completely change *your* life. You shouldn't want to get involved with me any more than I want to get involved with you. Which means we shouldn't even try to get to know each other."

She'd thought the same thing herself. Except her thinking had run along the lines of not being able to trust him. And hadn't she already figured out he had secrets? Though, it did intrigue her that he'd *admit* there were things in his life that prevented him from even considering a relationship. That had to mean there was more to his backing off than keeping his professional distance. Which was good to know. A woman who had been a little girl in foster care, wishing her next set of parents would love her enough to adopt her, didn't need to be wondering why he ran hot and cold with her or why he sometimes downright ignored her. Insecurities like that ran deep and popped up when she least expected, but his explanation tamed them.

She was glad she'd asked. Knowing would keep her from worrying every time he clammed up or ignored her. "Okay."

A laugh burst from him. "Okay?"

"Yeah. Okay. See how easy that was? You told me the whole story and now I understand all the weird things you've done since you realized who I was."

"I didn't do any weird things."

She raised her left eyebrow as she gave him an "Oh, really?" expression.

"Name one."

"Well, when we met, you talked a lot. Once you found out I was the person you were looking for, you barely said anything. In the diner, you were also kind of funny."

He laughed again. "*I* was funny?"

"Not hysterical but…" She shrugged. "You know. Silly?"

"My parents would not believe you if you told them that." He turned and started walking again.

She raced to catch up with him. "Which means I have to tell them. If only because they'll get a chuckle out of it."

"You'll probably never meet them."

She sighed. He was back to being careful again. She understood, but if they were stuck together for the rest of the day and he didn't talk, their time together would be insufferably boring.

"Are we really going out for dinner tonight?"

"Yes. One thing about New York City, there are a million wonderful restaurants I can take you to."

She glanced down at her worn jeans. She did have one dress packed. She'd planned on using it for the meeting with the lawyer, though. "Just don't get too fancy."

"Maybe we *should* go look for a dress?"

"I don't take charity."

"There's an entire slush fund at your disposal. That's not charity."

"You see things your way. I see them mine."

"Look, the bottom line is I don't want any attention being called to you. Neither does Danny. Dressing to fit in is a good idea." He pointed ahead of them. "There's a shop a few blocks down. It's where I get my mom's Christmas and birthday gifts. I'm going to have Danny set up an account for you. That way, after tonight, if you feel like you want a dress or shoes or something, you can get what you want or what you feel you need while you're here. No pressure."

"You want me to shop where you get your *mom's* clothes?" She laughed. "No thanks."

He sighed. "It's a nice place. It's got things for younger people, too."

"If you expect me to shop there, it better."

"It does."

She quelled the flutter in her stomach. She longed to look like the woman wearing the pencil skirt and silky blouse...but she also didn't have any money. Didn't have anywhere to wear something like that when she got home. Buying pretty things would be a waste. A waste of the money of a man who had hurt her. Money she didn't want—except to help her dad. She was only here on the chance she was an heir and she could help her parents. They were the ones who'd plucked her out of the system and saved her. She didn't need fancy clothes. Especially if she wasn't an heir.

"But don't get your hopes up. I'm not going shopping."

"You never know."

"I know."

"No. You don't."

She shook her head. For a guy who wasn't supposed to talk to her, he never seemed to let her get the last word.

CHAPTER FOUR

NICK TURNED TOWARD the entry of a grand hotel. Leni glanced up. A white facade was the perfect backdrop for the huge green wreath that sat above the portico. Red ornaments scattered around it glittered in the late afternoon sun.

The muscles around her heart tweaked. She was missing everything happening at home. Christmas parties, carolers, making cookies with her mom. Nick had told her to pack for two weeks and she assumed that's the longest she'd be away. She might miss the baking and extra-special holiday tips from regular customers at the diner, along with the occasional gift, but she'd be home over a week before Christmas.

There was no point in getting homesick. Everything was under control.

She followed Nick as he walked into the lobby, marched to the reservations clerk, gave his name and got a key card. Within seconds, they were in the elevator.

He continued the silence through the ride to

the tenth floor and down a quiet hall. When they stopped at a door, he opened it by scanning the key card. She stepped inside the room and gasped.

A huge window ran along the entire back wall, bringing the sights of Times Square into her room. Two red sofas sat parallel, in front of a marble fireplace with a bar off to the left. A dining table and upholstered chairs had been set up near the window.

"All this is for me?"

"Yes."

She looked around in awe. "This has got to be costing the estate a pretty penny."

"The estate has lots of pretty pennies, so don't worry about it." He glanced at his watch. "I'll be back at seven."

She nodded.

"If you need anything…and I mean *anything*, call the concierge."

"I do wish I had a book."

"I'm sure they can get you one."

With that he turned and walked out of the room, closing the door behind him.

She glanced around again. "No television." She spotted the big mirror above the fireplace, saw the remote on the mantel and laughed. "Thank goodness I watch enough house fixer-upper shows to know how they hide televisions these days."

She carefully lowered herself onto one of the

two red sofas, running her hand along the smooth leather, enjoying the luxury.

Was this how she'd live if she really was rich?

Even as she thought that, the silence of her suite enveloped her. She'd hate to think that all wealthy people were lonely. But Nick was rich...a simple billionaire he'd said...and he barely spoke. Of course, she knew why he didn't want to talk to her, but he didn't even speak to his driver.

That was what had bothered her. He never even said hello to his driver, the pilot for their plane or any of the ground crew scrambling to get their luggage into the jet's belly. He walked around as if he were in his own little world.

Which was a shame. Good-looking guy like that should be the happiest man around. And with all his money, he should realize he was one of the luckiest.

She thought of her adoptive dad. How he'd worked and scrimped and saved and barely made ends meet. Yet, he considered himself one of the luckiest people on the planet.

Nick Kourakis should be swinging-from-the-chandeliers happy and if she got the chance, maybe she would tell him that.

Nick arrived at Leni's suite at exactly seven. When she opened the door to him, he almost stepped back. His former elf wore a simple black dress with a red sweater. Her eyes had been painted with shadow and liner and mascara—but only enough to make her pretty, not overdone—and her lips were ruby red. Her long brown hair had been caught up in a twist in the back, giving her face a look of sophistication that nearly stole his breath. Black heels provided at least three inches of height and put her right at his chin. The perfect place for a woman to be.

He shook his head to clear it of that stupidity. She might be beautiful, but they'd never get to test out why coming to chin level was perfect. He would never kiss her.

That registered oddly, way deep down in his soul, in a place he hadn't acknowledged for so long the ping was a hollow, empty sound.

Calling himself foolish and exhausted, he ignored the weird feeling and said the one thing that might get her to tell him if she'd gone to the boutique after all. "You look nice."

"Nice?" She spun around once. "I look fabulous. This is the dress I'd bought for my college graduation ceremony last week. I'd brought it to wear to meet the lawyer, but I can wear it twice."

The hope that she'd shopped was replaced by another ping of acknowledgment in his soul. Her simple pleasure in the dress was fun. Almost cute enough to make him laugh.

He'd forgotten what it was like to really enjoy something ordinary. Actually, he'd forgotten what it was like to enjoy *anything*. He'd snuffed out that feeling, but one laugh from her and he remembered it, longed to feel it again.

Even though he knew he wouldn't.

He cleared his throat. "You made a good choice with the dress—and shoes."

She extended her foot and looked at her black pumps with love in her sparkling green eyes. "I know. They make me feel like I'm tall enough to talk to you without having to stretch my neck."

He'd thought they made her tall enough to kiss easily, naturally.

He really needed to get some sleep. The well-rested New Wolf of Wall Street didn't care about enjoying things, didn't compliment a woman he wasn't dating, didn't notice anybody's shoes.

But when Leni put on her worn leather jacket, he remembered her real world again. Remembered why this dress was so important to her. And told himself that no matter how tired he was, he could be nice to her.

Then she spoke. "You look pretty good yourself."

He glanced down at his black suit. "This is what I had on this morning." And the day before. It was a wonder he wasn't a wrinkled mess.

She winked and headed for the exit. "I know. You looked fabulous then, too."

His brain scrambled. Had she just flirted with him?

Realizing she was almost at the door, he had

to hurry to open it before she did, confusion and fear skittering along his nerve endings. They'd talked about this. There was no point in flirting.

He opened his mouth to remind her they'd already decided they shouldn't get chummy, which in his book included flirting, but as she stepped into the hall, she casually said, "I'm starving."

His brain stopped and then started again. She'd said he looked fabulous, but he hadn't confirmed that she'd flirted with him. And the "I'm starving" comment shifted them back to normal conversational territory.

Did he really want to bring up flirting?

Especially when they'd already discussed this?

Not in a million years. "Then let's get you some food."

Outside the hotel, at a time of day when the avenue should have been dark, it was lit by hundreds of thousands of lights from jumbotrons, video advertisements, scrolling newsfeeds and storefronts. Leni looked up and down the street, her curiosity and wonder evident on her face.

Nick suddenly understood why Danny had put her in Times Square. The place was filled with tourists and her interest blended with the curiosity of the people around her. Even if she couldn't control her reactions, she didn't stand out. Half the people on the sidewalk were gawking in awe at the lights and videos and shops.

"I hope you like Italian food."

Her eyes widened. "I love it."

"Great." He motioned to his driver that they were going to walk and headed down the street to the left. "I know a wonderful place. It's low-key. A favorite hangout of visitors to the city, most of whom are going to a Broadway play."

She huddled against the cold, sinking into her jacket, but her eyes were big, taking in everything in the exciting city he barely noticed anymore.

He slowed his pace, let her enjoy the walls of advertisements on the buildings, the vendors, the Christmas shoppers, and the cacophony of sounds from people and taxis and buses.

Seeing the city through her eyes, he felt the rhythm of it. The movement of tourists and vehicles in the brisk night air, all lit by thousands of colored lights.

The crowd thinned as they drifted away from Times Square. In another block they were at the restaurant. He gestured for her to walk down the black iron steps and opened the door for her when they reached the bottom.

Warmth hit him immediately, along with the shift in noise from a busy street to a crowded bar. After a clerk checked their coats, the hostess led them to a table in the middle of the dining area. The waiter poured wine for sampling. Nick almost told him it would be fine but realized he didn't even know if Leni liked wine. Mark had been someone who drank tequila with a beer chaser. Of course, her father hadn't been around to influence her decisions.

"Is wine okay?"

"Are you kidding? Wine would be great about now."

The waiter grinned, poured two glasses and scurried away, leaving them to read the menus.

She took a slow sip of the wine and savored. "This is fabulous."

He loved the way her eyes closed as she enjoyed her sip and slowed himself down as he took another taste from his glass. It *was* fabulous. "I think you're having a fabulous night."

She snickered. "That's pretty cocky of you to say."

"It's not me. It's you. You said you looked fabulous and I looked fabulous and now the wine is fabulous."

"Sometimes fabulous really is the only word."

He shrugged, but she was right. He'd known it when he took the time to savor the wine. He might not put himself or his clothes in the fabulous category, but her in that dress, with her green eyes and red lips? She was fabulous.

"Anything you recommend?"

He glanced up and saw her studying the menu. "Any of their pasta is—" he grinned "—fabulous."

She laughed. "You *do* have a sense of humor."

"No. I just took advantage of your love of fabulous."

"Nick?"

His brain stalled at the sound of his mother's voice, but he quickly gathered his wits and rose. "Mom!"

Leni glanced up at the pretty blonde with perfect makeup, wearing a bright blue dress, standing next to an older version of Nick. *His mom and dad?*

Nick's mom hugged him. "Sweetie! What a surprise."

"And what a surprise to see you," Nick replied.

Leni had to swallow a laugh. She'd bet it was a surprise…or a shock, from the horrified expression on his face.

He glanced at her, then said, "Leni, these are my parents, Amanda and Walt. Mom, Dad, this is my *friend*, Elenore."

She knew the emphasized word was for her. He wanted her to get on board with that description of who she was.

His parents looked at her expectantly. She didn't know if she should stand or stay seated or reach across the table to shake hands, and that lack of knowledge froze her.

His father nodded to her. "Nice to meet you."

"Nice to meet you, too."

His mother grinned broadly. "*Lovely* to meet you." She pulled in a satisfied breath. "You're here for dinner?"

Nick said, "Yes." He cleared his throat before cautiously asking, "Are you here for dinner?"

"We're done." His mother turned her big blue eyes on him. "You're lucky we're on our way to a play."

From the look on Nick's face, Leni would guess he did believe that made him lucky. But he said, "Too bad. We could have eaten together."

Leni almost snorted. She didn't think his parents bought that any more than she had.

His mother's gaze slid to Leni, then back to Nick. Her expression said she was putting one and one together—her son with a woman and not really wanting to eat dinner with his parents—and coming up with a very clear two.

"So, this is a date?"

Nick's mouth fell open slightly, as if he'd had to pause to stop the denial that automatically sprang up because he didn't know how else to explain who Leni was. He wasn't allowed to tell them the truth. Nobody was supposed to know who she was or why she was in New York. But she and Nick could be friends. All he had to do was stick with that.

Finally, he said, "I told you we're friends."

His mother laughed. "Friends could be on a date."

"Well, we're not. We're *friends*, having dinner together."

His mother turned to Leni. "He can be a real grouch sometimes."

The devil got into Leni and she smiled at his mom. "Oh, I don't know. The day we met he was actually funny."

Nick's mom's forehead scrunched. "Really? Nick was funny?"

Leni grinned. "Yes."

Amanda shook her head. "That's amazing."

Nick sighed. "Come on, Mom. I'm not that bad."

"Yes, you are." She faced Leni. "I'm hoping this means you'll be at the annual fundraiser Nick hosts for the children's wing of the hospital."

She glanced at him. "You host a fundraiser?" She wanted to say, "By yourself? Really?" But she suddenly realized that what was impossible in her world was probably commonplace in his. He'd have assistants and party planners doing the work.

"It's a thing we've always done. My dad's the one who's on the hospital board. I merely volunteer for this."

He sounded old and tired. About something he'd volunteered for...or something he'd been pressured into volunteering for?

"There's a Christmas party in the ward itself," his mother explained. "And an absolutely breathtaking ball a week later."

"Sounds nice." It sounded like a lot of work. On top of the job of running an entire company.

A company that had clients like Leni's deceased dad who had *billions* of dollars. If he'd given only half of that to Nick's firm to manage, that was a lot, lot, lot of responsibility.

His mom smiled. "I can see we're making my son uncomfortable and I don't want to ruin your dinner. But I do hope you'll come to the party and the ball."

"Yes," Nick's father said, but his eyes zoned in on her, studying her, judging her. "We would love to see you there."

No, he wouldn't. His tone said it quite clearly. But his mother was so happy to think her son was dating someone—Nick's denial had been too weak to shift her away from her hope—that guilt tweaked at Leni's conscience.

Knowing she nonetheless had to play along, she found a way to answer the question honestly without making promises. "I'd like that."

His mom smiled. "Great." She turned and headed toward the door.

Nick's parents walked through the small room packed with tables filled with diners and Nick sat down again.

Wanting to ease the tension, she said, "I told you I'd tell your parents you were funny."

"You shouldn't have. Now they're going to call tomorrow and ask a million questions."

"Look at it this way. I could have told them you flirted."

He cursed. "You are so lucky you didn't say that."

"Why? What are you going to do? Lock me in my hotel room?"

He rolled his eyes, but she could see she'd shifted his focus, and if she kept teasing him maybe he'd relax.

"Your mom sure likes the idea that you might be dating someone. Have all your other dates been shrews or has it been so long since you've dated anyone that she all but did a dance of joy?"

"It could be a combination of both."

She chortled. "My mom and dad do the same thing. Except they tried to set me up with every eligible guy on my dad's construction crew." She took a breath. The last two years had been so difficult with her dad being injured that she'd forgotten that, and the memory sent a wave of sadness through her. "But he hasn't worked in two years." She sucked in another breath. And she hadn't had a date in two years.

She was in no position to tease Nick.

The waiter arrived. They ordered. As he'd said, the food was better than anything she'd ever eaten. Preoccupied with enjoying every bite, she almost didn't notice that they didn't talk. They finished a bottle of wine and refused dessert, which meant the night was over. And she would go back to the hotel now.

Stepping out into the quiet end of the street, she

let herself enjoy the city. She didn't mind returning to her room. It was cold and she had warm pajamas in her suitcase. Plus, she was tired. It had been a long day.

But with Nick silent beside her, she thought about his parents again and her guilt over deceiving them returned. His mom was expecting "Nick's friend" to show up at a hospital event when technically she was in hiding.

Because he hadn't told them the truth.

"Do you lie a lot?"

His voice jerked with surprise. "What?"

"I understand keeping your distance from people and not talking to your driver and pilots and such, but you seemed to lie really easily to your parents."

He shook his head. "I did not lie. I led them to draw their own conclusions. And what my dad ended up thinking is going to cost me a lecture because I can't tell him who you really are. But I did try to steer them away from thinking we were dating."

"Yeah, but you did it a little too late."

"I had to leave a little doubt in their minds because we're hiding you, remember?" He sighed. "It's just better if I keep my distance."

Complete disbelief overwhelmed her. "With your parents?"

"Especially with my parents."

She glanced over at him, but he was staring

straight ahead. No expression on his face. No remorse. No sadness. No sign of guilt.

"Now, see? To me that is just plain odd. After a year in foster care I was so grateful to get parents that I'd never want to be distant."

He pulled in a heavy breath. "Have you forgotten we decided it would be better if we didn't get to know each other?"

"We're not talking about ourselves. Technically, we're talking about our parents."

"That's worse. That could be construed as me trying to get your sympathy."

"Because you don't date?"

He dropped his head to his hands. "My not dating isn't reason for anyone's sympathy. This estate must be handled carefully. Danny wants to be the one who explains all this to you because there's a lot at stake."

She mumbled, "I suppose," and shut up. The beauty and noise of Times Square were enough to take her attention for the rest of the walk. Ambling through the lobby of her hotel to the elevator, she didn't expect him to talk.

But when they reached her door, the silence seemed out of place. She said the only thing that popped into her head. "I had a great time."

"What? Not a fabulous time?"

And her Nick was back. The guy she liked. They might have agreed not to get too chummy, but his "fabulous" comment was definitely flirting, at the very least teasing. Still, what would a little flirting hurt? It wasn't like stoic Nick Kourakis would fall in love with her because she teased him.

"Just not going to let me forget that, are you?"

He laughed. "No."

Their eyes met and suddenly it felt like a date. Not the weird outings she had with guys her dad found, but one of the real dates she had the first few years at university. Dates with guys who thought her pretty, made her laugh and wanted to kiss her.

Her heart sped up. What if *Nick* wanted to kiss her?

He couldn't...could he?

Why not? He'd flirted with her. And before that he'd told her she had a warmth about her that was appealing—all but admitted he liked her when he explained why their getting to know each other was a bad idea.

The silence continued as they gazed into each other's eyes. He was gorgeous, funny sometimes, and he'd taken good care of her that day.

If he did want to kiss her all he had to do was bend forward a few inches and press his lips to hers—

Her heart nearly exploded just thinking about his mouth meeting hers. She could not let her thoughts run away from her like that! She couldn't forget that Nick wasn't her friend because he didn't want to be. It would be crazy to spin fantasies about someone who'd told her up front he didn't want to get involved with her. She'd had enough rejection in her life. When she chose a romantic partner, it would be someone who didn't have secrets, someone who'd trust her and love her, just as she was.

What it felt like to kiss Nick was totally irrelevant stacked up against the truth of what she needed. She shouldn't be probing into his life or, worse, spinning fantasies about him.

She turned and swiped her key. For the first time since she heard the no-talking rule, she realized it was a wise one. "Good night."

CHAPTER FIVE

LENI WOKE THE next morning totally disoriented.

In a fancy hotel, fighting a crush on a guy with secrets, she ordered eggs and toast from room service and a pot of coffee.

When her breakfast arrived, she grabbed her cell phone and called her mom.

Her dad answered. "Hey, Kitten."

"Hey, Dad. Feeling okay?"

"Fit as a fiddle." He always said that, not wanting Leni or her mom to worry. "How's the Big Apple?"

"Huge. Except it goes up to the sky instead of spreading out."

"Oh, it spreads pretty far. Your mother's tapping my shoulder. I think she wants a turn."

Before Leni could say goodbye to her dad, her mom said, "So? What's happening?"

She told her mom about eating on the jet, riding in a limo, seeing people dressed in fancy clothes, going to the Italian restaurant and how Nick didn't want to talk about the estate because the lawyer needed to explain it all to her. He couldn't.

She bit her lower lip. "It's all kind of strange and confusing. Like I'm in a dream."

"In a way you are."

"Yeah, except I can't shake the weird feelings I have about Mark Hinton. About him having money and letting my biological mom struggle, especially when she was sick."

"Powerful men do things the rest of us don't understand."

"I suppose. But inheriting his money feels wrong…" She paused to think that through then said, "It feels sleazy."

"Sleazy?"

"It's almost like I'm so thrilled at the prospect of getting money that I'm letting him off the hook for abandoning me and my poor mom." She didn't mention that no one had seen her biological mom since she had given Leni up. Her mother knew that. When Leni was sixteen, they'd hired an investigator to look for her but never found her. They also never found a death certificate. That meant her mom had survived whatever illness she'd been fighting when she had to give up Leni. But she'd never come back for her. Hadn't even checked up on her as far as Leni knew.

That's the thing that haunted her sometimes. Her mother hadn't seemed to want her any more than her biological father had.

"But we need this money for dad. It's the worst rock and a hard place. Taking this money feels like I absolve everybody of not wanting me."

Her mom's soft sigh drifted through the phone. "Oh, Leni. Don't you remember how much your dad and I wanted you? We'd tried for years to have a child and couldn't. When the social workers put your little hand in mine, my heart melted. You brought so much joy into our lives."

She did remember. Mostly because she was eight, not a toddler, not an infant but a kid who understood what was going on. "You guys made me very happy, too."

"Because we were so grateful to get you. Your biological parents might have left you, but we were desperately happy for the privilege of raising you."

As always, her soft-spoken mother's words were like a magic balm. Still, there was something very basic about being rejected not just by a mother who didn't come looking for her after she got well, but by a guy who didn't want her at all.

And the money felt like the key. Almost as if, if she refused it, she would shake off her feelings of rejection forever. But just when she would convince herself that walking away was the right thing to do, she'd remember her sick dad and hesitate.

Would she be selling her soul, the way she

viewed herself, the code of honor she didn't even realize was so strong, if she took that cash—even if it was for her dad, not herself?

Nick knocked on Leni's hotel room door that afternoon to take her for a stroll through the Metropolitan Museum of Art. Danny had called to say his trial had not ended, and when Nick asked for specifics, Danny mumbled about the length of testimony of witnesses being way over what Danny had thought they should be. But he swore the trial would finish up the next morning.

Nick had sighed and agreed to entertain Leni. Not because he felt for Danny but because he felt for *her*. She was a nice woman in a strange city, here to ascertain whether she was the heir of a huge estate, but the vetting process hadn't started because Danny wasn't available to do his job.

Nick was positive that after a morning of being cooped up, she'd be eager for even his company, but when she opened the door, she wouldn't meet his gaze.

His heart stuttered. They were right back where they were when he'd brought her to the door the night before. One minute they were practicing safe silence walking down the hall to her suite, and the next they were making flirty comments and gazing into each other's eyes. Then she'd broken the contact and run into her room.

While he'd been standing there thinking about kissing her.

What was it about being in front of a door, saying good-night, that brought out that instinct? Or longing. What had trembled through him wasn't just a desire for a kiss. It was more. Something part of him wanted but the other part knew he couldn't have.

But she'd raced off. She'd handled the moment perfectly—getting them both off the hook.

So why wouldn't she look at him now? And why wasn't she talking? She always talked. Even when he reminded her that they shouldn't.

"Where are we going?"

Her quiet, impersonal question might be talking, but it wasn't typical Leni chitchat.

Maybe she finally realized it really was better if they didn't get to know each other? Didn't veer off into conversations that tempted him to kiss her—

"I thought I'd take you to the Metropolitan Museum."

She slid her purse strap onto her shoulder as she faced him. She wore her scruffy jacket and jeans, but the Met was filled with all kinds of people. And she looked nice. She didn't need fancy clothes to be attractive.

"That sounds great."

"I think you'll enjoy it." And they could talk as much as she wanted—about art. The Met was the best way to allow her to be chatty and use up a lot of time happily, neutrally. He was a genius for coming up with it.

Silence reigned as they rode the elevator to the lobby and walked out onto the street and into his limo.

Accustomed to her talking, the quiet enveloping them felt wrong. But he told himself not to worry. She wouldn't be able to contain herself at the Met. Plus, her not talking on the drive worked to his advantage. The questions she asked always drew him in even though he knew it was wrong. He kept falling into the feelings he'd had at the diner, the instant connection. The almost-kiss at her door the night before proved it.

She didn't say a word on the limo ride, while she climbed out of the car or even on the busy street in front of the Met. But she also didn't look around the way she normally did. She kept her eyes fixed on her old boots as they ascended the steps into the museum. Her gaze stayed lowered as they walked inside.

He hated this.

She was much too perky and sunny to keep her head down and herself quiet. But that was why he'd brought her to this enormous museum. There was plenty to talk about without once getting personal. He just had to nudge her to recognize it.

He glanced around, saw the exhibit housing

the Christmas tree and smiled. That would get her talking.

He guided her to the Medieval Sculpture Hall. Her head came up slowly and she gasped at the enormous Christmas tree. "Oh, my…"

"It's a twenty-foot blue spruce." Glad he'd skimmed the information as they'd walked in, he directed her to the base of the tree where a full nativity scene was arranged beneath the lower boughs.

But her gaze stayed on the upper branches. "The angels look like they're climbing to the sky."

Proud he'd realized she wouldn't be able to resist talking about the gorgeous Christmas tree, he rocked back on his heels. "Or coming down to earth."

She stepped a few feet to the right, examining the figures scattered about the tree and shook her head. "It's the most beautiful thing I've ever seen."

He angled his head toward the door. "There's a whole building full of wonderful things. There's even an armor room. Egyptian art. Modern art. What do you like?"

Her smile returned. "I don't know. I've never been anyplace like this."

He motioned to the exit. "We have five hours to look your fill."

She headed for the door. "What happens in five hours?"

"I take you back to the hotel to get ready for dinner."

"Out?"

"Sure. If you're worried about what to wear, the account at the boutique has been set up for you. All you have to do walk in and give your name."

Her spine stiffened. "No, thank you."

"Seriously? You have access to money while you're here. Just take the limo to the boutique and use the account."

"You make it sound so easy."

"It is."

"When you have money."

Her statement was flat with a hint of bitterness, and he almost stopped walking. Locked in those few words was the reason for her unhappiness. He was certain of it. But he didn't want to be curious about her life any more than he wanted her to ask about his. He had parents to please, a brother who was gone and sorely missed, a difficult life that a good person like Leni shouldn't get dragged into.

He squelched the troublesome questions about why she might be so sad through two exhibits, but eventually he began going over everything she'd said the day before until he remembered how she'd reacted to his misleading his parents, especially her reasoning. She'd been confused by him distancing himself from his mom and dad because she'd spent a year in foster care—

That nagged at him until he couldn't stand it anymore, and his question was out before he could stop it. "Were you really in foster care?"

She turned away from a bright painting. "Yes. I was seven when my mom put me in. Eight when the Longs found me and adopted me."

Her answer brought him up short. *She'd been abandoned by her mom? In foster care for an entire year before she'd met the Longs?*

"That's tough."

"My mom couldn't keep me because she was sick. Her choice was to feed me or buy medicine." She shook her head. "My dad was a billionaire, but my mom was too broke to save herself and care for me, and she made the only choice she could. I ended up living in three different homes with three families I didn't know." She paused, caught his gaze. "It was the worst year of my life."

His heart hurt for her. There was so much sadness in that simple explanation that a longing to comfort her rose up in him.

But that was a slippery slope.

He shoved his hands into his pockets. "You know what? Let's just move along. Maybe work our way to the Egyptian exhibit."

"Okay."

The cloudiness was back in her eyes and Nick sucked in a deep breath. He'd probably been a little too abrupt changing the subject. But if he hugged her to comfort her, his brain wouldn't stop there. He'd feel her softness. Her curves. Get drawn into the strange connection he'd had in the diner, the feeling of warmth and comfort and rightness that had washed over him. He'd want things he couldn't have. Romance and connection required honesty, and he couldn't be honest with anyone, couldn't talk about his mistakes, didn't want anyone to see or know the real him.

Out of necessity, his life was nothing but business but hers could be about to change dramatically. In a very good way. And maybe he should help her realize that?

"You know, you might be surprised when you talk about the estate with the lawyer. If you're an heir, your life will change so much for the better."

She said, "You think so?" Then she peeked at him. "Is *your* life better?"

Though the question hit him right in the heart, he laughed. "Better than what?"

"The average person's?"

His little white lie was automatic. "Of course."

"Really?" She frowned. "You barely talk to your parents or your staff. I'm guessing you live alone. And the one thing you do that seems like fun—plan a ball—is probably organized by your assistant."

He scowled. "Do you always have to question everything?"

"Hey, I took a lot of psychology courses. I know what I see."

"I'm happy." In his own little way, he was. He'd built this life, this world, this persona to protect himself. And as long as he was safe, he was fine.

"No. You're not. Not even close. Take this museum," she said, motioning around them as they headed for the next exhibit. "While I'm actually looking at things, enjoying them, you're watching me. But not because you're interested in me. Because you're responsible for me and you think I'm a ticking bomb. Like any minute you expect me to explode."

"You have done some pretty weird things."

She stopped so she could stare him down. "Such as?"

"Tell my mom I'm funny."

She laughed. "Has it really been so long since you've made normal conversation that you've forgotten what it sounds like?"

"I talked to you at the diner."

"Yeah, you told me Mannington seemed like a nice town. That led me into talking about my job search. Which led you to tell me about your family business—and having a rebellious streak." She stopped, gave him a quick once-over. "Huh. I guess you do know how to hold a conversation after all."

She walked away, heading for a set of stairs. "There's an exhibit up here I really want to see. Because that's what people in museums do. They examine things. Then they discuss them. You should try it."

His footsteps echoing around him, he scrambled after her. Not to talk, though she was right. Talking about the exhibits was why he'd brought her here. But now that she'd pointed it out, he felt odd about talking. Every time he was around her, his reasoning got jumbled. His best intentions went straight to hell. His safe little world shook a bit. She didn't have the power to tear it down, but she could sure shake it.

She led him to the European paintings exhibit and honestly even if he'd wanted to talk, he wouldn't have. A reverent hush fell over them as they looked at work dating back to the thirteenth century. His breathing slowed as he studied landscapes and sunsets, blue skies and children. Knowing artists painted what they saw, he recognized he was looking at the world as it was hundreds of years ago.

"You're feeling better now, aren't you?"

He glanced at Leni. How was she so damned right all the time? "Yes."

She shrugged. "I'm really good at what I do."

And now she read minds? Answering questions he hadn't asked out loud? The woman was going to drive him insane.

Leni walked away glad she'd said her piece, but also enjoying the art. For as much as she knew the European exhibit would have a calming effect on Nick, she'd also known it would center her. She didn't want to rush her decisions about Mark Hinton's estate or jump to conclusions, and with the lawyer unavailable she had nothing but time to think about things.

She was glad Nick had brought her here. Not just for something they could discuss without consequences, but because sometimes all it took to get perspective was seeing the world through another person's eyes. Especially if that person lived in another century and their world was so different from her own.

They walked around the museum for the promised five hours, commenting on the exhibits sometimes but mostly staying silent, then Nick said it was time to go. She surreptitiously glanced at her watch. Five hours exactly.

She almost sighed. She didn't mind a person who loved precision, but he would take her to the hotel and then return to pick her up for dinner and he'd be careful about everything he said. If fun Nick did make an appearance, it would be short-lived.

It was getting old.

Just as she predicted, they stayed quiet on the ride to her hotel, and even on the walk to her room. With fun Nick nowhere to be seen, she didn't even think about a kiss good-night. But it wasn't really night. It was late afternoon. He had the entirety of their dinner that evening to sit stonily beside her. It was getting kind of insulting that he wouldn't talk because he didn't think it was appropriate for them to get to know each other.

Well, guess what? Neither did she. She had absolutely no desire to get to know grumpy Nick.

Frankly, she'd rather read a book.

She slid the key card over the lock, but as the door clicked open, she faced Nick again.

"I know you'd mentioned going out to dinner tonight, but I'm tired."

He frowned. "What?"

"I'm tired. It's what happens to people when they walk around for five hours straight. I'm going to order room service, put on my pajamas and watch some TV. Maybe I'll call that concierge guy and see if he can get me a book."

He stepped back, seeming totally confused. "Okay."

She supposed she didn't blame him. She had the whole of New York City at her disposal and she'd rather stay in. Not because she didn't want to see the city but because she didn't want to see it with a guy who didn't want to risk getting to know her.

It was weird, tiresome. Who the heck did he think he was, anyway? Did he think if he talked to her, she'd instantly fall at his feet in adoration?

She might be from a small town, but she wasn't brainless.

"I'm fine. Just in the mood for some me time. Don't worry. I'll be here tomorrow."

She entered her room feeling like herself for the first time in days. Not just because seeing the wonderful exhibits had centered her, but because she'd made a logical choice.

She didn't have to be bored with gorgeous Nick Kourakis. She could read a book.

Nick stared at her closed door. Okay. He had to admit his ego took a direct hit when she'd said she'd rather stay in and read a book than go somewhere with him. There had been a time when he was the most fun, most interesting guy on the planet. Women lined up to spend time with him. Not one of them would have preferred a book.

Walking to the limo, seeing the Christmas decorations that signaled the season of peace on earth, he stopped, glanced around. They *were* amazing.

He hadn't noticed things like Christmas decorations since Joe died. Being with Leni was opening his eyes again. Not because she was pretty, though that certainly didn't hurt. But because she was so damned transparent and honest. He knew her experience in foster care and then being raised by two loving parents played into that. Not to mention small-town living. He supposed if there were only fifteen hundred people in your entire town, life would be very different. She'd seen the good and bad side of the world, of people. Comprehended things only someone who'd gone through trouble could appreciate. And she had a degree in psychology.

Actually, she'd probably understand *him* if he told her about his situation.

Shaking his head, he started toward the door of his limo again. She'd love that. She'd already evaluated him in the museum, basically told him he was boring then refused dinner with him.

He hated that that bothered him so much.

But it did, and he wasn't sure why. He'd think it was because he didn't like being rejected. Except, this wasn't personal. They'd already decided to keep their personal feelings out of this. He only had to babysit her, entertain her, when she'd been left alone too long.

So why did her rejection skim along his nerve endings, a constant reminder that wouldn't go away?

He got into the limo and stared out the window at the lights and people on the drive to his Park Avenue penthouse. He rode the quiet elevator that opened onto his stunning open-plan home, stripped off his scarf and tossed his overcoat on the sofa to the sounds of silence. Cold, hollow silence. The same silence that greeted him every night.

She was right. New Wolf of Wall Street or not, he had become boring.

He walked past the seating arrangement, pool table and bar to the windows in the back and looked out at the city dressed for the holiday. Now that he was noticing the decorations again, he remembered how much his brother had loved Christmas, remembered their childhood Christmases. How Joe had spent months finding the right gifts for everyone, wrapped them with care and sat with bated breath while everyone opened their presents—

The cold, hollow silence morphed into sadness. He missed his brother. He'd never felt it before because the guilt was always stronger. But tonight, he missed Joe. Missed him with the kind of ache that took ahold of his heart and squeezed until his eyes drifted closed.

He wondered what Joe would be like now, and knew they'd still be best friends. He felt the loss again. Thick and all-consuming. The weight of it on his shoulders made him pull in a long breath. In some ways, the guilt was better. Guilt pushed him to work, to not let their parents down. This sadness only hurt.

The ring of his phone burst into the quiet. He considered not answering, but knew he had to. He was his parents' only child now. If something was wrong, he had to be there.

He yanked it from his pocket, scowled at the caller ID and said, "Hello, Danny."

"Hey, Nick."

"I hope you're calling to tell me your trial ended today."

"No."

Nick sighed. He'd suspected as much, but it had been worth a shot.

"There are two more witnesses." Danny's voice wobbled in that weird way voices sometimes do when someone has something difficult to say. "We should wrap up tomorrow but if not tomorrow definitely on Friday. No one will want this thing on hold over the weekend."

"But that's not a guarantee."

"No. Sorry. Honestly, this opposing counsel has confused me at every turn. I have no idea what she's going to do next. For all I know, she might only have one question for each of the last two witnesses. But even if the trial is still going on Monday, I'll have the weekend off and I'll be able to talk to Elenore on Saturday. You'll be off the hook with her."

Relief poured through him, but he winced. Leni was one of the nicest people he'd ever met, and he was acting as if being with her was a chore.

It wasn't. Fighting his attraction to her was the chore.

He sat on the edge of the pool table. He'd told

her that. Told her they shouldn't talk. Been a real jackass about reminding her of that.

All because he liked her.

Danny broke into his thoughts. "So, can you give Leni a little time out of the hotel room tomorrow?"

He'd never had a problem like this with a woman before. If he wanted someone he usually went after her. But Leni was different. She would soon be a client if she decided to keep her share of her dad's money with his management firm. And she was a nice woman who didn't deserve a broken heart from a man who only did one-night stands.

But that didn't mean he had to be a jerk. When he'd told her that they shouldn't talk, shouldn't try to get to know each other, he hadn't realized they'd be together so much. Now that he knew, he needed to shift his strategy.

And maybe he should be glad he had another day or two to make up for being an idiot.

He thought for a minute about how he'd go about doing that, then smiled.

"Yeah. I can entertain her tomorrow."

"Okay," Dany said. "Just remember not to talk about the will or the estate."

Nick laughed. The woman had called him boring. The last thing he wanted to discuss with her was a will, an estate or his job. "I can promise you the will and the estate will not come up in conversation."

He hung up the phone feeling much better. He'd taken the no-talking thing a step too far, but now that he'd figured that out, he could make it up to her.

Tomorrow he'd show her he could be a fun guy.

CHAPTER SIX

THE NEXT MORNING, the ring of her cell phone edged its way into Leni's dream about waiting tables at the Family Diner, giving out free Christmas cookies, getting big tips and saying "Merry Christmas" as she waved to customers walking out the door.

The phone rang again.

With a gasp, she sprang up, off her pillow. Confused to be out of the dream so suddenly, it took another ring before she grabbed her phone. "Hello?"

"Good morning, Leni."

Nick.

She couldn't stop the happiness at hearing his voice any more than she could stop the ripple of annoyance. She could spend 24/7 with the Nick who made her laugh, but she didn't want to spend another long, boring day with the guy who didn't want to talk.

She carefully said, "Good morning, Nick."

"Danny's stuck in his trial for another day."

And she and Nick were stuck together for another day—unless she could sway him into thinking she didn't need to be entertained? "I haven't even gotten out of bed yet. It could be a lazy day for me. It's fine that Danny's not available."

"No. It's not. It's incredibly unfair that we're keeping you in New York and not getting on with the reasons we brought you here."

Who was this guy? The Nick she knew was either funny or grouchy. Never accommodating. "Don't worry about it. I can read a book today."

"No, your being stuck here is an imposition. So, to make up for that, I thought we'd do something really fun today."

"I'm okay with getting a book and just vegging today."

"You vegged last night. Today, I thought we'd go skating at Rockefeller Center."

Her breath hitched. She sat up a little farther on the bed. *"Rockefeller Center?"*

"It's gorgeous when it's decorated for Christmas. And they have an enormous tree."

Her entire body longed to do something physical, but more than that she loved to skate. With her busy schedule and her dad's troubles, she hadn't skated in the past two years.

Excitement filled her blood, boosted her mood, made her not care that Nick Kourakis wouldn't say a word beyond what he had to. As long as she had skates on her feet, it didn't matter.

"I love to skate."

"Good. Get your breakfast and put on something warm. I'll pick you up around ten."

"I'll be ready."

She threw aside the covers, called room service and got her shower. By the time she had herself wrapped in one of the hotel's big white robes, her breakfast had arrived. She tried not to gobble because she had until ten, but it was useless. Everything she'd done since arriving in New York had been foreign to her. Today, she would do something she loved.

In the bedroom, she pulled out two pairs of socks, her warmest jeans, a T-shirt and a sweater for over it. She applied a little lip gloss and mascara, but when it came time to do her hair, she decided against pulling it into a bun or a ponytail. She loved the feeling of her hair floating around her when she skated. She curled it but kept it down.

She returned to the sitting room just as there was a knock on the door. Opening it, she found Nick.

"Ready to skate?"

Instead of his usual suit, today he wore jeans, a thick sweater and a dark parka. With his hair just a little messed and his eyes bright, he looked young and carefree.

And happy.

If she didn't know better, she'd think he was as excited to go skating as she was.

Maybe ditching him the night before had made him realize he needed to loosen up? Maybe because he liked her?

Remembering that's exactly why he didn't want to talk to her, she stopped that wishful thinking. There was something between them. Attraction, sure. But it was more. There had been a connection that he didn't want. If she called his attention to it, he'd turn back into grumpy Nick. The guy she didn't want to be around.

On the way down in the elevator, he said, "Did you sleep well?"

"I'm finally getting accustomed to not being in my own bed."

"Good. I slept well, too."

His unexpected small talk caused her to give him the side-eye, but the elevator door opened, and he guided her outside to his limo. They seated themselves and the long car slid into traffic.

"How was your breakfast?"

She frowned. The guy who didn't want her to be chatty was chatting. Again. Still, she wouldn't be rude or, worse, call attention to it.

"I had toast and eggs. Hard to screw that up."

"That hotel is known for its restaurants." He glanced at her and smiled "Maybe we should eat there tonight?"

The smile jump-started her heart and scrambled her pulse. She told herself to settle down because this kind of reaction was exactly what Nick didn't want.

Schooling her face into complete neutrality, she said, "Yeah. Eating at the hotel would be great."

The limo fell silent, but within a few minutes, they arrived at Rockefeller Center.

As Nick had said, the huge Christmas tree dominated the area, and she had to stifle a gasp. Lit by what looked to be millions of lights, it sat in front of the Rockefeller Center building, with a backdrop of other tall buildings. Angel statues with trumpets sat by the tree. A row of flags created a wall. At least fifty people were already on the ice.

She stepped out of the limo feeling like she was stepping into a fairy tale. "It's beautiful."

It was also a perfect day, cold but not freezing. A blue, cloudless sky smiled down on them. No wind. No snow and lots of sunshine.

"I think this is my favorite place in New York City."

No longer surprised that Nick had spoken, she sneaked a peek at him. He glanced around the space as if seeing it for the first time. She could tell from the expression on his face that he didn't intend to be a spectator. He wouldn't stand behind her watching her like a bodyguard or stalker. He wanted to be here.

But not for *her*. He was only entertaining her. If he liked this place it was because it was gorgeous and filled with fun. And she was desperate for a little fun.

Maybe he was, too?

"I can understand why it would be your favorite place. It's wonderful."

"It is."

They paid the fee, rented skates and were on the ice in what felt like seconds. With a quick push off, she skated in a big circle to get the feel of things, then eased back to him. He clearly liked this place. She liked to skate. Having something physical to do was exactly what they needed.

"Come on! Skate with me."

He stood there, looking gorgeous in his parka and jeans, but also unsure. "I haven't skated since my teens."

When he'd bring his brother.

The thought shot through Nick's brain as bright as the sun glistening off the ice. Joe had loved skating nearly as much as he'd loved Christmas.

Nick almost groaned, thinking it had been a mistake to bring Leni here—except he wanted her to have fun. Real fun. This was a place to have fun.

"You came here as a kid?"

He shrugged. "Yeah. By the time I was a teenager I was a great skater."

That made her laugh. "Conceited much?"

"It's only conceited if you talk about it all the

time." Finally feeling comfortable enough on his skates to try them out, he eased his way to the far wall then back again. When he reached her, he skated a ring around her.

"Very funny."

"I keep telling you I'm not funny."

"So that was a sarcastic ring you just skated around me?"

"It was more of a proof ring." He grinned at her. The sky was blue. The world was dressed up for Christmas. And he was on skates.

For the first time in five years he felt Christmas in the air. The wonder of it swirled around him, along with a magic he didn't quite understand. Maybe because Leni was back to teasing him? Maybe because she no longer seemed quiet or careful? Maybe because she was back to her old self?

Tonight, he would nurse his remorse about his brother, but this afternoon he would not think about Joe. He would show Leni a good time and demonstrate to her that he was a fun guy in an unromantic way that would ease both of their nerves about what a jerk he'd been about not getting to know each other.

"Wanna race?"

He took off before she had a chance to answer, bobbing and weaving around other skaters. She saw a clearer path and took it, beating him to the wall.

"Ha! I win."

"You probably skated last week. So, you're on your game."

"Nope. Haven't skated in two years."

He shrugged as he made a small circle around her. "Give me another ten minutes and no one on this ice will beat me."

"How do you get through doors with that big head?"

He laughed, breathed in the air again and something inside him stilled. He'd brought her here to have fun and instead he was the one laughing.

"Race you to that wall." The second the words were out of her mouth she was skating away.

A lover of competition, he pushed off immediately and his longer legs had him beside her in seconds. "I'm going to beat you."

"Who says?" She blew past him and was at the wall before he drew three breaths.

He reached her and said, "One more time," before he shot off.

She burst after him, passed him and stood with her arms folded on her chest when he finally caught up to her.

"How do you do that?"

"What? Beat you?"

"You have short legs."

She laughed. "You have a fat coat." She caught a chunk of the material stuffed with down, but when she looked up at him to say, "It's not aerodynamically sound," they both realized she was touching him. Like a friend, sure. But they weren't friends. They barely knew each other—

Except they had that damned connection they'd made at the diner the day they met. She'd been cute and funny, and he'd been instantly smitten. They'd spent two days together and she'd made him laugh as well as made him crazy. And after Danny talked to her on Saturday, he'd only see her in his capacity as her money manager.

That didn't sit right. She was too different to like, a part of his job and a royal pain in the butt with her honesty, but the thought of never laughing with her again, casually, naturally, seemed so wrong it sent confusion rippling through him. He wanted this day, maybe *needed* this day to laugh with her, as much as she did.

She let go of her grip on his parka and jerked her hand away, but he caught it before she could put it down to her side. "Let's just do a few laps."

"Why?" Shielding her eyes from the sun with a hand nestled in bright green mitten, she said, "So, you can get your form back?"

That was as good of a reason as any. "Yeah." Was it so wrong to want to have fun with her? He hadn't had fun since Joe died and maybe that's why his subconscious had brought them here. He'd missed Joe the night before. And being here now made him remember his brother in a good way. Not the painful way that had enveloped him before Danny called.

She pulled her hand out of his, skated a circle around him. "When you were a kid, did you do tricks?"

He sniffed. "Like a trained dog?"

"Like someone imitating Olympic skaters."

She executed a perfect toe loop.

He applauded.

"Now, you do a trick."

"I didn't do tricks when I skated. I just raced."

"Raced?"

"My brother. So, I'd win, and girls would like me."

She frowned. "Your brother?"

His mention of Joe stunned him as much as it stunned her. He would have pulled back the words if he could, but they were out there now, and he wasn't sure why.

"He was only a year younger than me." He said it easily, casually, so she wouldn't make a big deal out of it, testing the words, trying to figure out why he suddenly wanted to talk about Joe. "We'd race. I'd beat him. And girls would flock after me."

She shook her head. "You have really got to do something about your ego."

She did another two toe loops and pushed off to get speed enough for an edge jump.

Nick watched her, his heart in his throat. He'd

skated to get girls, but she skated for the pleasure of it and watching her was pure joy. Nothing he'd ever experienced. Something as mesmerizing as it was wonderful.

He eased over to her and took her hands, so they could skate sideways in a circle.

"This is your big trick?"

"I told you. I don't do tricks. I only skated to get girls."

She chuckled, let go of his hands and raced off. He followed her, caught her and grabbed her hand again. This time he twirled her under his arm. She spun gracefully, tilting her head back, letting her long hair fall behind her and looking like poetry on ice.

His heart swelled with longing. Of all the women in the world, why did he have to like the one he wasn't supposed to like?

She owned a big chunk of the money his company was managing. But more than that, she was one of the nicest people in the world and he was a man filled with guilt and remorse.

He didn't deserve her.

When she stopped, she said, "So tell me more about your brother."

His chest pinched. He longed to tell her about Joe. Years had passed with him holding all this inside, and she was the one person who would understand.

Actually, that was the point. Her sweetness,

her honesty made him want to open up. And he shouldn't. A man like him should let a nice girl like her alone.

"I'd rather race."

At first, she looked confused, then she smiled. "Okay." She pointed at a spot on the wall. "I'll be there two seconds before you."

He laughed and pushed off after her. He might not be the right guy for her, but that didn't mean he couldn't enjoy her company.

Just this one day.

CHAPTER SEVEN

HAVING MISSED LUNCH, they decided to have an early dinner at an Irish pub rather than at her hotel. Happy from skating, Leni glanced around excitedly as they entered. The place was dark, partially because of low lighting, but also the walls were paneled with dark wood. The floors were dark. Blinds covered the windows. Even the shiny bar was dark wood.

"It's like a hideaway."

Nick laughed. "You have a weird way of looking at things."

"Oh, I don't know. Maybe I look at things the right way and you're the one whose perception is skewed."

He shook his head as they approached the hostess. The restaurant was empty except for an older couple at a table in front and two men at the bar. The bartender, a beefy guy with dark hair and a ready smile, gave them a quick once-over and Leni suspected he was also the bouncer. She didn't miss the glance that passed between him and the hostess and she realized they were in love.

Her heart stuttered as she saw they both wore simple gold wedding bands. Without saying a word, they communicated the kind of love and commitment that anyone who looked at them would know would last a lifetime.

The hostess guided them to a little table in the back and Leni smiled her thanks before the young woman made her way back to the bar area. Leni caught the bartender's wink and the hostess's smile and her heart could have melted into a big pile of goo.

She peeked at Nick, who was engrossed in his menu, realizing he hadn't seen any of it. Two things hit her immediately. First, she was in some sort of fanciful mood because of skating. Second, a few hours of fun had changed him. He laughed easily. Held her gaze when they spoke. And suggested this lovely little bar for dinner. Like friends. Not a guy stuck with babysitting her.

They sat with their menus for only a few seconds before a waitress appeared. They both ordered a beer and she scurried away.

"See anything you like?"

She lowered her menu to the table and winced. "Just fries."

"You can't live on fries."

"So, my mother says but I've always wanted to test that theory."

"You shouldn't. You need protein, too."

She grinned devilishly. "I had protein at breakfast. This isn't a permanent rebellion. Just a little skirmish."

"I'm feeling a little skirmishy myself."

She'd already figured that out and peeked at him. "Really?"

"Yeah. You get the loaded fries. I'll get the classic margherita flatbread."

"And we can share!"

"My thought exactly."

The waitress arrived with their drafts and they ordered their appetizers. She walked away, and Leni leaned back in her chair. Fun Nick was here and better than usual. The weird connection that had popped up at the oddest times since their meeting at the diner seemed to be gone, but happy Nick was much better.

"I like it here. It's sort of like a bar back home but it's cleaner."

He laughed. "Did you go there a lot?"

"I thought I wasn't supposed to talk about my life? You know, because it's pointless for us to get to know each other."

"Let's just say that things changed a bit. Besides, we've spent so much time together that we have to start talking about something or we'll die of boredom."

Totally onboard with that assessment, she sat up. "What do you want to know?"

He shrugged. "I don't care. Tell me about school."

"Well, scraping the money together was hard but I didn't want to be one of those people who graduated owing more money than I'd ever be able to pay back."

He smiled and nodded, and she shook her head. "Look who I'm telling. You don't understand debt."

He winced. "Sorry. I don't."

"I like that you're honest about that."

"I think you're starting to rub off on me."

She laughed. "Wouldn't that be something."

"Yeah. I just can't figure out if it's a good or bad something."

"What kinds of things are you picking up from me?"

"Your over-the-top honesty, for one."

She took a sip of beer. "That's a good thing. What else?"

"Saying things that pop into my head."

"That's all part of being honest."

He shook his head, but he also took a breath and glanced around. "It *is* comfortable in here. Reminds me of my old life."

"Old life?"

He looked down, played with his silverware.

"Yeah, before I took over the family business, I traveled a lot. Went to places like this."

She might have wondered about why he seemed to be avoiding her gaze, except she'd never traveled, and she gasped excitedly. "Like Irish pubs in Ireland?"

"Exactly like that."

"Is that why you don't notice your surroundings or the people?" She waited a beat then said, "You've been so many places that this is dull to you?"

"Not dull. But I've lived in this city my entire life. I've seen every restaurant and street. I'm kind of accustomed to it. Going to Yale was a nice change of pace."

Happiness filled her. When he was normal like this, she could just take his cheeks between her palms and kiss him. She reminded herself that she shouldn't. Not merely because grumpy Nick could make an appearance any second but because he'd warned her he didn't want a relationship. Though she could enjoy herself, she would keep her emotions under control.

"You went to Yale?" Having expected Harvard, Yale was a pleasant surprise. "Really?"

"Nothing wrong with Yale."

"No. No. Yale's a great school. So, what was your rank?"

He winced. "I was the top of my class."

She didn't doubt that for a second. "Then you went to…"

"The Navy."

Expecting him to tell her about post-grad work, she flopped back on her chair. "What?"

"By the time I was twenty-one I had had it with sitting in classrooms and writing papers. I joined the Navy, discovered the SEALs and the challenge was too hard to resist."

"The challenge?"

"I love a challenge."

"I want to save the world and you love a challenge."

He laughed at her. "You think saving the world isn't going to be a challenge?"

"I wasn't planning on making any big moves. Just saving one person at a time."

"That's nice."

"I thought for sure you were going to say that's naive."

"I've known you long enough, Leni, to realize that you probably get just about anything you set your mind to."

"My dad always said I was like a little dog with a bone." Thoughts of her dad struggling at home hurt her heart, so she said, "Tell me about being a SEAL."

"It was amazing." He caught her gaze. "Changed my life. Everyone thinks of the world through a specific set of beliefs. Going into the military shows you just how big and how troubled the world really is."

"And?"

"And?"

"Is that what made you unhappy?"

He shook his head. "Being a SEAL, being on active duty, gave me a sense of purpose. But when my time was up, I knew I'd seen things that messed up my thinking a bit. I wasn't ready to go home, but I couldn't shirk my family responsibility anymore."

She gaped at him. "Are you telling me becoming a SEAL was your *rebellious* streak?"

"Yes."

She shook her head. "And you tell me I have a skewed vision of life."

"You do. And I don't. Not really. My parents wanted me involved with the firm. Becoming a SEAL only delayed that, but it was a rebellion."

She nodded thoughtfully. "So, after the SEALs you settled down and took over the family business."

"No. After the SEALs, I was antsy and couldn't stay in one place long, so I had to figure out a way to do my duty and give myself a chance to process my time in the military. In the end, I told my parents I'd be something like a recruiter. I traveled the globe and looked for investors like your dad. After a few years of bungee jumping and skydiving with risk takers like myself, I grew the firm from being moderately successful to being one of the top firms on the planet."

She could only stare at him. She'd never in a million years have believed he'd done so much. And most of it dangerous. "Wow."

The waitress came with their food. The conversation died as they poured ketchup, cut the flatbread, asked for refills of their drafts.

She took a bite of flatbread and groaned. "Oh, this is fabulous."

"My fabulous girl is back."

Her heart skittered. He'd called her his. Even if he meant it in the most generic of ways, those words tumbling off his tongue filled her with joy. Which was ridiculous. She'd known him only a few days. And he'd very clearly warned her that he didn't think it was a good idea for them to even consider a relationship. She told her heart to settle down, but the reminder was good. Fun Nick was very hard to resist, but she had to.

They ate and laughed some more. The bar got darker, as if reflecting night falling on the street outside.

The waitress brought two more drafts. Nick talked a bit more about the jet-setting he'd done to find new clients, and she stared at him. He had to be the most interesting person she'd ever met. He knew and was friends with kings, princes, billionaires, tech geniuses.

He could have talked down to her. He could

have bragged. Instead, he just talked. As if they were friends.

The power of it made her breath catch. He was better educated, more experienced, more refined, cultured, sophisticated than she could ever dream of being. And it was pretty damned hard to remind herself that she was nowhere near a match for him when her overeager heart just wanted to be with him. Even if it wasn't forever. Even if it was just for tonight.

After one more draft, they slid into their coats, walked past the busy hostess and bartender who still had time to exchange smiles and stepped onto the street. With the sun down, the brisk air had chilled even further. It seeped through her coat and made her shiver.

She slid her arm beneath Nick's and huddled next to him for warmth. "I hope the walk to the hotel isn't a long one."

He laughed. "It's not."

He tucked her hand against his chest and she all but melted. He might not mean anything by what he was doing, might not even notice what he was doing, but he was stealing her breath, changing her idea of Prince Charming and making her wish she could be the kind of woman he'd be interested in.

They walked through the hotel lobby laughing but drifted apart in the elevator.

At her door, the distance between them annoyed her. But what was she going to do? Fix his collar just so she could keep her hands on him?

"Thank you for a really great day."

"Figured I had to do something since you all but called me boring yesterday." He shook his head. "You'd rather read a book than spend another two hours with me?"

A laugh escaped. "I didn't mean it like that."

"Of course, you did." He stepped close, put his hands on her shoulders and slid them up her neck, under her hair. "You have such beautiful hair."

And him touching it sent a rain of glittery awareness from her scalp, down her spine. "Thank you. I always figured my hair was God's way of making it up to me that the first few years of my childhood were awful."

Her voice had come out soft and breathless. She didn't care. She wanted him to hear the shiver of awareness, wanted him to bend down and kiss her. She wanted their mouths to meet, their tongues to twine and the glittery sprinkles to go from a gentle rain to a torrential downpour.

"I had a good time today, too."

She smiled, giving him as much of a hint as she possibly could that he should kiss her—without embarrassing herself or ruining something about this night, this minute.

He closed his eyes and took a breath before pulling his hands away. "Thank you for today."

"You're welcome."

He could probably see the disappointment in her eyes because he'd stepped away from her. "Depending on Danny's schedule, I might see you again tomorrow."

And he didn't want to kiss her tonight if they had another day together. She understood that. Kisses were acknowledgments, invitations or endings. An acknowledgment kiss was a way of saying *I like you*. The invitation kiss said *I like you and this might go somewhere*. The ending kiss said *we had fun, I like you, but this can't go anywhere*.

He could have given her the acknowledgment kiss.

He could have given her the invitation kiss, knowing her inheritance could ease her into his world and, even if Danny was free the next day, they could see each other again on their own— if he wanted to.

The only kiss he couldn't give her was the goodbye kiss. Especially not if they had another day with him entertaining her.

No matter how much he liked her. No matter how much fun they'd had that day. No matter how right they seemed when they were together—

He didn't feel the same way about her as she felt about him. Otherwise, he would have kissed her.

She took the step back this time. She'd already

realized that, though he was attracted to her, she probably wasn't his type. She wasn't a sophisticate. She hadn't been top of her class. She hadn't traveled the globe. A smart woman didn't long for a man so different from herself, a man with secrets.

And she knew he had them. She'd guessed it all along. The fact that he wouldn't tell her was a proof of sorts that what she felt pulsing between them wasn't going anywhere.

She slid her key card along the pad. "Good night."

"Good night."

In her room, she shrugged out of her jacket, tossed it on a chair and then peeled off her sweater.

She was so disappointed that her heart felt bruised. That confused her. She had accepted that she wasn't right for him—

So why did she still want that kiss?

One kiss.

It might not be good to wish for a lifetime with a guy whose world was so different than hers. But there was nothing wrong with wanting a kiss.

Was there?

Hell, no.

The guy was great, gorgeous…fun. She was allowed to want a kiss.

Tomorrow night, at her door, he wouldn't have to wonder if he'd see her again, wonder if she'd still be in his charge. No matter what happened, Danny would take over on Saturday morning.

She had one more day to get that kiss.

Then she'd go back to being a client or a customer or nothing, if she wasn't an heir. In which case, she'd be returning to Kansas and she'd never see him again—

Yeah. She wanted that kiss.

CHAPTER EIGHT

THE FOLLOWING MORNING, Leni's cell phone rang while she was eating breakfast. Seeing the ID for Waters, Waters, and Montgomery, her heart sank.

Noooo.

If that was Danny Manelli calling, his trial was over. She wouldn't see Nick that day—maybe not until the estate was settled, when she'd be his client—if she decided to keep her share of the money with him. When things would be all business.

There'd be no kiss.

Taking a breath, she told herself not to jump to conclusions, clicked the screen and said, "Hello."

"Good morning, Leni. This is Danny Manelli. You and I haven't officially met, but I'm the lawyer for the Hinton estate."

Desperate hope quivered through her. Maybe he was calling because he had something to tell her? Maybe he wanted to apologize for not being available all week? She knew there could be nothing between her and Nick, but she'd wanted that one kiss.

"I know who you are. Nick gave your card to my parents. I saw your name. But Nick has also mentioned you."

"My trial is over. This morning we can finally begin the process of me explaining a few things to you. We'll also get the DNA samples."

Her throat closed. Damn it. This *was* it. The end. She'd never see fun Nick again. From here on out he'd be the boring businessman, if she saw him at all.

She worked to keep her voice even as she said, "Okay."

"I can have a limo there in forty-five minutes. Is that enough time to get ready?"

"Sure."

She disconnected the call and immediately went to the spa-like bathroom to shower. She refused to cry. Yes, a kiss would have been wonderful. But maybe that would have made things worse? Whatever his secrets, Nick obviously couldn't give her what she needed. A real relationship. A strong relationship with no guessing, no possibility of rejection. And maybe kissing him would have drawn her in so much she might have tried for more with him when more wasn't possible?

She had to let her fantasy of a kiss go.

This was for the best.

She had herself believing that until she pulled her black dress out of the closet. Pressing it to her face, she closed her eyes. She'd worn this to the Italian restaurant. They'd had wine, great food and she'd met his parents.

She popped open her eyes again. That had been one of the best nights of her life. But she wasn't a simpleton. Lots of things separated her and Nick. Including the fact that she didn't know his secret. No matter how sweet, how funny, how kind he could be…something in his life was terribly wrong. She'd known it even before he'd mentioned it.

In her internships, she'd counseled women to stay away from men with secrets. Bad boys. Wouldn't she be foolish to fall for one herself?

When the elevator doors opened on Danny's office, her suspicions about not seeing Nick were confirmed. The tall, dark-haired man wearing a white shirt, black tie and black suit pants was the only person in the room. As she stepped out of the elevator, he rose from the big desk, extending his hand to shake hers.

"I'm Danny Manelli, Leni. It's a pleasure to meet you."

She slid out of her old, worn coat. "It's nice to finally meet you, too."

After she was seated, Danny called in a lab tech who took three DNA samples. One for his lab and two for random labs. With that out of the way, the attorney went on to explain that she was potentially one of three heirs and the estate was in the process of looking for the other two. That was all she needed to know until they confirmed she was an heir.

"But once you're confirmed, you'll have access to your share of the money."

She thought of her adoptive dad's needs and nodded.

"So, now we wait for DNA to come back before you either go home if you're not an heir, or before I set up some bank accounts for you."

"Okay." She got quiet. With four days to think all of this through and acclimate, it wasn't as overwhelming as it had been on Monday or Tuesday. Refusing her dad's money wouldn't be cutting off her nose to spite her face. Especially since her new plan was to ask for the child support her dad had never paid. But this wasn't yet the time to talk about that.

"Do you have any questions?"

"Not about the estate."

"Good." Danny relaxed against his seat as if satisfied with her reaction. "Do you have something to ask that's not about the estate?"

"Yes." She glanced up at him. "Can I go home?"

Danny shook his head. "That's tricky. Do you want to go home and risk being mobbed?"

"Why would I be mobbed? My parents and I haven't told anyone about this. As far as I can tell no one knows who I am or why I'm here. So, I'm still anonymous."

Danny tossed his pencil to his desk. "It seems iffy to me."

"It doesn't to me, and I want to go home, to talk about this with my parents. I don't want to sleep in a bed I don't know and run around Times Square looking like a bumpkin when I'm not. In Mannington, Kansas, I'm a normal person. I want to go home."

She also didn't want to miss Nick. To walk down the street and see things that reminded her of him. Once she got home, she'd be fine. She was sure of it. The whole time they were together, she'd been smart enough to keep her wits about her. Going home would be like wiping the slate clean.

Danny studied her for a few seconds. "All right. I'll arrange it."

Nick went to his office on Friday morning and was inundated with messages and meetings. With a little persistence and focus, he was able to clear the things that only he could handle before noon. Which left him with his usual work.

When he returned from lunch, his assistant closed the door to his office, giving him total privacy. He settled himself on his big desk chair intending to buckle down, but with his brain cleared, his thoughts jumped to Leni.

Skimming his hands through her hair the night before was a terrible luxury he couldn't resist. He'd really wanted a kiss, but that was one step too far. He'd known there was a chance Danny would be free today and he wouldn't see Leni again as anything other than a financial manager. Kissing her would only confuse her—especially since he didn't want anything growing between them. Then he'd touched her hair and tripped something inside himself. Not merely a sexual attraction, their connection. The feeling that there was something between them.

But he'd already decided this. She was a wonderful person and his life was dark, bleak. He had regrets that made him moody. Work that kept him sane. He wasn't right for a fun, happy person like Leni. Not even to date.

He forced his mind to the prospectus in front of him, knocking her out of his thoughts, but before ten minutes were up, she had tiptoed into his brain again. By now she would have spoken with Danny. He knew that because Danny had told him she'd be in his office that morning, they'd do a DNA sample and he'd explain some things about the estate to her.

He didn't think she'd be overwhelmed. If anything, she probably felt like she had some answers. So, she was fine.

He took a breath, put his attention on the prospectus and managed to work twenty minutes before he wondered what she was doing that afternoon.

Not that she needed a babysitter. It was just that the city could be intimidating—

No. He'd taken her around and watched her handle herself in some pretty weird situations this week, including meeting his parents.

That made him laugh, then he groaned. He had work to do.

He focused again and he made it until four o'clock when his phone rang. Seeing Danny's name in the caller ID, he jumped on the phone.

"Hey, Danny. How did it go with Leni?"

"Really well. She's very sweet and accommodating and smart, but we have a bigger problem."

Nick sat up. "Problem?"

"I got a call from her mom. Her dad's been taken to the hospital."

His breath stopped. "What?"

"Her dad's in the hospital, but that's not the worst of it. Leni asked if she could go home. After making her promise she'd keep a low profile, I got her a flight to Topeka."

Though his heart skipped a beat out of concern for her, Nick forced himself to relax. "She'll be home where her parents need her."

"Nick, her dad's in real trouble, but her plane has already boarded so her phone is off. She's going to fly to Kansas and go home to an empty house. Her mom said she didn't even have time to leave a note."

"She won't drive home. She'll call her mom when she lands."

"Phones aren't allowed in ICU. But even on the off chance that her mom would be in the cafeteria when Leni calls her, do we want her to find out that her dad's in ICU, maybe dying—in a phone call? When she's at an airport, with no car and no idea how to get to the hospital? We can't do that to her. Someone has to meet her at the airport and tell her this."

Leni was the sweetest, nicest person in the world. Nick absolutely could not let her go through that.

He scrubbed his hand across his mouth. "If I take my jet, I can beat her commercial flight to Topeka."

"I know. That's why I called."

"Then you also know I don't have a minute to spare."

He said that as he gathered work to shove into a briefcase. If he would be in the air for three hours, he could at least get some reading done.

And not obsess about seeing her again, or worse, acknowledge the way his heart lifted with relief that he'd get more time with her.

Leni deplaned, happily saying buh-bye to the flight attendants and heading up the ramp to the gate. She raced to baggage claim, her phone in her hand as she called her mom. Again.

It wasn't a surprise that no one answered at the house, but her mom should answer her cell phone—

Nope. It went straight to voice mail, as if she had it turned off.

After a few minutes, her small bag came down the chute and rolled along the conveyor belt. Before she could grab it, someone behind her did.

She spun around to tell the man he had the wrong suitcase but found herself face-to-face with Nick.

Her heart stumbled. Crazy scenarios filled her head. Like he'd heard she'd left New York without saying goodbye and he couldn't have that.

Not letting herself give into a foolish wish, she said, "What are you doing here?"

He drew a breath. His usually serious eyes were even darker than normal. "Your dad had a problem."

It was the last thing she expected him to say and she fell back a step. "What kind of problem?"

"A major seizure. That's all I know. Your mom called Danny when she couldn't get ahold of you because you'd already boarded your flight. Danny sent me to get to you before you rented a car and drove to your empty house." He nudged his head toward the exit. "I've got a car and we can drive straight to the hospital."

She stared at him. It was the second time in a week he'd given her news that simply couldn't connect to her brain.

But this news filled her eyes with tears. "Is he all right?"

Nick solemnly shook his head. "I don't know. Let's not think the worst. Let's drive to the hospital, talk to your mom and see what's going on."

She nodded and they headed in the direction of his rental. Using GPS, they found the hospital. The information desk told them that her dad was in ICU and her mom was with him.

When they arrived on the floor, her mom came out of his room and fell into Leni's arms.

"It was the worst thing. One minute he was laughing and the next he had zoned out. I thought it was a longer-than-normal small seizure but then he started shaking and he fell to the floor. I called the ambulance immediately."

"You did the right thing," Leni said soothingly. "How is he now? Can I see him?"

"You can see him, but it took so long to get the seizure under control that he's heavily sedated and sleeping. He hasn't even moved in hours."

"I'll feel better if I see him."

Her mom nodded and turned to walk Leni into the ICU, but she noticed Nick and stopped. "I'm sorry. I didn't even see you there. Nick, right?"

"Yes. It's okay, Mrs. Long. I'm fine. I'll find a seat out here. You two go ahead."

Leni's mom nodded and guided Leni back to the ICU. In a hospital bed, with an IV and hooked up to several monitors, her dad looked awful.

Leni's mom put her arm around Leni's shoulders. "They told me that a grand mal seizure like that takes a lot out of a person and with the sedatives he could sleep through the night."

Desperate for confirmation, Leni looked at her mom. "They're sure he's okay?"

She pointed at the monitors. "That's what all those bells and whistles are for. As long as none of these alarms sound, he's fine and he's not having another seizure."

They stayed in the room and watched her dad sleep for at least a half an hour. But sitting in the plastic chair, the stress of the day caught up with Leni. She yawned.

"You should go home."

"No, I'm fine."

"You're not fine. You're tired." Her mother's head tilted. "Didn't you have a meeting with the lawyer today?"

"Yeah. He told me the bare bones about the estate. That everything had to be so hush-hush because there's tons of money and then said he couldn't tell me anything more until they got the results of the DNA test that prove I'm an heir."

"You don't seem to be upset anymore so it must have been good news."

"Yeah, mostly good." She still had the decision about how much of this money she'd take, if any, but she wouldn't share that with her mom until her dad was home and healthy. "The thing of it is, if I am an heir, I think have to hire my own lawyer because Danny stressed that he's the lawyer for the *estate*. I know that means he's not looking out for me but for the estate.

"He also said my DNA samples had to go to the labs blind. Meaning no one could know they were for the Hinton estate. Even though Waters, Waters and Montgomery put a rush on them, no one could say when the results would be back. So I asked if I could come home." She grimaced. "I'd wanted to surprise you."

"Instead, we surprised you."

Nodding, Leni looked lovingly at her dad. What she wouldn't give for him to wake up and make a corny comment.

"Still, there's no reason for you to be here. He won't be up till morning. Go home. Get some rest."

She glanced at her mom. "Are you staying?"

"Of course. There's a pullout bed I can sleep on."

"Then I'm staying, too."

"And sleep on one of those plastic chairs in the waiting room?"

"I'm too nervous to sleep." Then she remembered Nick was with her and she sighed. "I'll send

Nick to a hotel. Better yet, I'll send him back to New York. Do you have your car?"

Her mother nodded. "I followed the ambulance."

"Good. He can take his rental back to the airport and fly home."

She walked out into the waiting room and Nick bounced from his chair. "How is he?"

"Sleeping. Heavily sedated, so they think he won't wake up until morning."

"Is that good or bad?"

"Mom said the doctors told her this kind of seizure takes a lot out of a person and sleep is what he needs."

"Then that's good," he said hopefully.

She drew in a long breath. "I guess."

"Sit down."

She lowered herself to a tall-back, padded double chair big enough for two. As he sat beside her, she said, "Now that I'm here, you can go."

He looked at her incredulously. "Fly back home?"

"Or just get a hotel."

"Are you going to a hotel?"

She gazed at the door separating the ICU from the waiting room. "No. I don't think so. Mom's staying until morning. I will, too."

"Then I will, too. The chairs aren't too bad. We might even be able to get a little sleep."

"I'm too drained to argue." She leaned back,

relaxing a bit. "But at three o'clock in the morning when your back aches, you might change your mind about these chairs."

He laughed. She nestled into the seat, getting more comfortable. With only the two of them in the waiting room, it got incredibly quiet when they stopped talking.

Her mind going in a million directions, she steadied her breathing to settle herself. Then she sniffed a laugh. "I remember the day I met my parents."

Nick shifted to face her. "You do?"

"Sure. I was eight by the time they got me as a foster child, so I knew exactly what was going on."

"It must have been hard."

"Being in foster care at all is hard. But it was scary too, going with another set of 'parents.' The Longs explained that they wanted to adopt me, and I was shocked."

"Why? I bet you were a cute little kid."

"Every foster home I went to, I had the ridiculous belief that these people would love me enough that they'd keep me." She met his gaze. "No one had."

"You didn't want to get your hopes up."

"But the Longs were so eager to please me that they were actually funny. After a day or two of my dad bending over backward to make me laugh or feel comfortable, I realized my forever home *was* with them. These people who always made breakfast and liked to play Yahtzee were mine forever. I decided to be the best child ever and I had a wonderful life with them."

"That's a great story."

She smiled. "I know." But the truth of where she was and what was going on washed over her and she squeezed her eyes shut. "I could not handle it if my dad died."

"He's not going to die."

"We don't know that."

Her raw fear came through in her voice and helplessness overwhelmed Nick. He leaned forward, across the double chair, and wrapped his arms around her. "We might not *know* but we can hope."

She nestled into him for comfort and he held her close. He understood her fear of having someone she loved die. He could not bear watching her go through it.

They dozed a bit, woke around three o'clock and she checked on her dad. Ten minutes later, she came back to the waiting room.

"I talked to the nurse. Everything's the same. My mom is sleeping."

Nick stretched. "That's good."

She sat on her chair again. "Yeah." This time when she settled in, she used her jacket for a blanket. Nick did the same with his big gray overcoat.

They must have dozed again because the next thing Nick knew, they were cuddled against each other, his big coat covering them both in the cold December air, and light was streaming in through the big windows of the waiting room.

He just held her for a few seconds, savoring the feel of her. He might not deserve anyone as good as she was, but if he could give her strength or courage, he would. She was a tough person, but she'd already gone through too much in her short life to have her dad die—

He couldn't fathom it. He knew how death hurt, how it ruined things, how it raced like a scourge through a family.

He took a breath to stop his runaway train of thought and when he looked down, she was gazing up at him.

"Hey."

"Hey." He couldn't protect her from this, but he would do the one thing he could do. Support her.

"We should go into Dad's room to see how he is and if my mother survived the night on that rock-hard sofa bed."

He laughed and released her, but his silent vow remained intact. He would do whatever she needed.

They walked into her dad's room to find him sitting up in bed. Her mom sat on the edge of the foot of the bed, grinning from ear to ear.

Leni raced to her father and all but threw herself into him to hug him. "Dad!"

"Hey, Kitten. Better loosen the hold."

She jerked back. "I'm sorry! Did I hurt you?"

"No. But I am a bit stiff and sore." He winced. "Weirdly stiff and sore. When I get home, I'm going to have you research seizures so I can see what this one did to me."

"Or we can just do a few tests."

The doctor standing in the doorway walked into the room. "I'm Doctor Stevens. I'm your neurologist. I've been looking at your chart and see you had a work injury."

Leni's dad nodded. "Two years ago."

"And these seizures are just manifesting now?"

"I started having small seizures a few months ago." Her dad grimaced. "That might not be true. I'm told the smaller seizures could have started long before I noticed them."

The doctor made some notes. "Let's get some tests before we make any assumptions."

He left the room and a few minutes later a nurse appeared. "I hear you're getting some tests this morning."

She looked at his wristband, asking his name, double checking. "Tests will be at least two hours." She smiled at Leni's mom. "Go get some breakfast." Without waiting for an answer, she took Leni's dad away.

Leni said, "We should do that, Mom." She

glanced at Nick, silently asking for his help convincing her mom. "I know I'm starving."

"I could use something myself," Nick agreed.

But Leni's mom sighed. "I couldn't eat."

"You should eat."

She shook her head. "No. You guys go. Bring me back a cup of coffee."

Leni argued a few seconds, but eventually gave up. "If you're not going, I'm not going."

Nick said, "How about if I go find coffee and maybe some doughnuts?"

Leni sent him a grateful smile. "That'd be great."

It took him fifteen minutes to find the cafeteria but only a few seconds to realize he didn't know if Leni or her mom wanted cream or sugar for their coffee. He got a cardboard container, put three disposable cups of coffee in the slots then filled the fourth slot with creams and sugar packets. The clerk put six doughnuts into a bag, and he headed back to ICU.

He found Leni and her mom in the waiting area, seated at a round table. He passed out coffee and opened the bag of doughnuts, letting Leni and her mom choose first.

"It's all so frustrating," Leni's mom said before she took a long drink of coffee. "One minute he was fine. The next he was gone. No warning."

"That's what the service dog is for," Leni reminded her mom.

"We can't afford—" Leni's mom paused, smiled at Nick. "Sorry, don't want to air our troubles in front of you."

Nick shook his head. "Hey, no worries here. Every family has troubles."

He thought of his mom, who'd thrown herself into charity work after Joe's death, and his dad, who'd thrown himself into checking up on Nick, making sure he stayed put, making sure he made money for the family—his silent way of reminding Nick he had to make up for losing his brother.

"Besides," Leni said, taking a napkin from the stack by the coffee container, "we might not have anything to worry about financially. Even if all I take is what my father should have paid in child support, it'll be enough for Dad's medical bills."

The conversation died after that and though Nick should have wanted to ask Leni a million questions about potentially walking away from billions of dollars, he felt oddly proud of her. She had principles and guts. But she also wouldn't abandon her father.

A strange feeling tingled through him. The certainty that he should be here collided with the knowledge that being with her wasn't right. What if he gave her the wrong impression? What if he influenced her—

He almost laughed. Leni would call that notion conceited. She'd ask him how he got his head through doors.

Helping her in her time of need would not give her the wrong impression. She was level-headed and smart.

And he could handle himself, too. Yes, they'd gravitated together in the middle of the night. Yes, it had felt wonderful to hold her. But half-asleep, he'd forgotten he needed to keep his distance. Now that he was remembering, he could help her without getting close.

When Joe died, he'd forced himself through some of the worst emotions a person could feel. He could help her while protecting himself.

CHAPTER NINE

WHEN HER FATHER returned from getting his tests, the nurse suggested that they all needed to be rested when the neurologist arrived that evening to discuss the results. Leni agreed and she convinced her mom to come home with her to get a nap.

She rode in the car with her mom and Nick followed them in his rented SUV. They arrived at the Long home an hour later. Though the day was cold, the house was toasty. A batch of sugar cookies, coated in frosting and covered in red and green sprinkles, sat on the counter as if her mom had just finished making them when her dad had his seizure.

Denise removed her coat and hung it on a coa-track by the door. "Let me make lunch."

Leni gaped at her mom. "No!"

"Absolutely not," Nick agreed. "You heard what the nurse said. She wants you rested when you come back."

Denise shook her head. "I'm too keyed up to sleep."

Leni put her hands on her mom's shoulders and turned her in the direction of the bedrooms. "Go lay down anyway."

"I'll tell you what," Nick said. "You get some rest and when you wake up lunch will be ready."

Leni faced him. She might not have seen Nick's life, but she would guess he had a maid or ate out most of the time. He certainly didn't look like a guy who knew how to make lunch. "You're going to cook?"

He laughed. "I'm not a great cook but I make a mean spaghetti."

Denise half smiled. "I like spaghetti."

"Good. Go rest."

As her mom walked away, Leni studied Nick. When he wanted to be, Nick Kourakis was the nicest guy in the world. He'd picked her up at the airport, taken her to see her dad and stayed with her and her mom, not just getting coffee and doughnuts but offering moral support. And she couldn't forget how they'd moved close together in the night, snuggling together for warmth. And how he'd been studying her face when she'd awakened—

But she remembered he also hadn't kissed her at her hotel room door the night he could have. The night it would have been the perfect ending to the perfect day, he'd walked away from the chance to kiss her. And despite the way they'd cuddled together in the chilly waiting room, he'd told her Danny had called him to let him know about her dad and asked him to fly to Kansas to intercept her. His being here was Danny's idea. Gravitating together for warmth meant nothing.

"I'm not sure we have spaghetti in the house."

He shrugged. "Does Mannington have a grocery store?"

"Of course, we have a grocery store!" Realizing she'd protested too much, she winced. "A small one."

"As long as it has spaghetti, I don't care if it's the size of a minivan."

She laughed, as she re-zipped her jacket. He really knew nothing about small towns. But her mom needed support and Nick was offering it.

Because Danny had sent him.

As long as she remembered he was only here because Danny had asked, she wouldn't make too much of him being here and wouldn't get stars in her eyes.

"Let's go."

They headed outside to the SUV. Leni got in the passenger's side and Nick slid behind the steering wheel. Understanding the significance of Danny having sent him, she wouldn't lean too heavily on him. She would accept help caring for her mom. But that was it.

Apparently misinterpreting her silence, he said, "Are you worried about your father?"

Thinking about her dad and everything he

might have to go through made her tired suddenly. She put her head back and closed her eyes. "No. I'm coming to terms with everything. Remembering things."

"Remembering things?"

"When he first started having seizures, I looked them up."

He laughed.

She sniffed. "You laugh, but the internet can be very effective. Especially when it says that most seizures aren't life-threatening."

Nick waited a beat then said, "His new, longer ones might be."

"I don't think so."

"You sound pretty sure of yourself."

"Not sure of myself, but sure of my dad. He's like a bull when he wants to be. It was hard seeing him weak when he was injured, but now he's back to being himself or wanting to fight whatever is going on, and to me that's half the battle."

Nick tilted his head. "Maybe… Which way is this store?"

She pointed right. He made the turn. The Moe's Market sign appeared about a block down.

He pulled the SUV into a parking space and they went inside. Leni grabbed a cart. He smiled stupidly.

"What?"

"I've never been in a store like this."

"Like what?"

He pointed toward the seven aisles of food and household products. "You think this is small. To me it's enormous."

"You mustn't have ever been in a superstore." She pushed the cart toward the fresh produce. "How deprived you've been."

He chuckled. "I think you're the first person who's ever called me deprived." He glanced around in awe. "Look at all this food. Especially the Christmas candy."

She studied the bright red, green and gold boxes of chocolates, candy canes, right beside red felt stockings. "Giving candy as a Christmas gift is very big around here." When she saw he was still staring at the boxes, she laughed. "Do you want to take a box or two home?"

He nudged his chin to the right. "Not candy, but maybe a few bags of potato chips."

She chuckled as she stopped by the lettuce. "Are you making a salad?"

"Do you want a salad?"

"We always have salad with spaghetti."

"Good to know."

Her eyes narrowed. He'd said that as if he planned on remembering it. But why? "Are you taking notes?"

"No. I just like knowing things about people for future reference."

His words slid through her. She tried not to conclude that he might be staying in her life—

especially with their differences so clearly spelled out as he looked at her town's very ordinary store with wonder in his eyes. But when he was so personal, so helpful, so easy with her, the thought drifted through her brain anyway.

He casually grabbed the handle and pushed the cart up the aisle, toward the tomatoes, while Leni stood frozen by the lettuce. To her, it felt like he belonged with her. Weird as it seemed, they were good together.

She shook her head to clear it. She could *not* think like that. If Danny hadn't called him about her dad, she wouldn't have seen Nick after Thursday night—until it came time for his company to make a pitch for her to keep her Hinton inheritance in his money management firm. She couldn't fool herself into thinking he had feelings for her.

For pity's sake, they'd known each other five days. Six if she counted the current day. She'd stayed at three different foster homes *for months* and each time she'd walked in one day after school to be told to pack her bags and get ready to move on. She could still feel the sting of it. The horrible sense that she wasn't loveable. And she'd vowed she'd never let herself feel that again.

If she could be rejected after months with foster parents whom she believed liked her, six days was nothing.

Especially not a reason to set herself up for a rejection.

Where was her pride?

Where was her spunk?

She wasn't one of those women who fell for a man who wanted nothing to do with her. She was independent and in her own little small-town way, savvy.

Still, she grabbed a few bags of the potato chips he liked and met him at the end of the aisle.

"Any chance there's fresh bread here?"

She motioned to the left. "There's a bakery section down there." Then she laughed. "I'll bet some of your clients would pay to see this. I'll bet your *mom* would pay to see this."

He scowled. "I'm not helpless at doing normal things because I'm wealthy."

"Sure. Sure."

"I'm serious. I was a Navy SEAL. I know how to do things."

Confused about how being a Navy SEAL would help him make spaghetti, she tilted her head as they walked to the bakery section. "Like what?"

"Do you want to hear about the killing-a-man-with-my-bare-hands part or the how-to-survive-just-about-anywhere part?"

She stopped, gaped at him. "Did you actually do those things?"

This time he gaped at her. "What do you think

being in the SEALs means? That they let me sit on a couch and watch TV while the other guys went on missions? I passed muster. I was part of missions to capture people and part of missions to rescue people."

She knew her mouth hung open, but she couldn't stop staring at him.

He put his fingers under her chin and closed her mouth. "Seriously."

"I'm sorry but it just all seems impossible." Or did it? He was a big guy. When she'd first seen him, she'd thought he had the comportment of someone in the military. And he'd told her he liked adventure…danger.

"What else did you do?"

"Classified stuff. So, don't ask."

By this time, they had all the makings of salad, spaghetti and meatballs and two jars of sauce. "I'm going to start cooking as soon as we get to your house. I want the meatballs to be ready when your mom gets up and she might only sleep an hour or so."

She nodded casually but she was in awe of him, the way she'd been when they walked out of the Irish pub. The day she'd slid her arm under his and snuggled into him as they returned to her hotel.

After ringing up the sale, Tilly Montgomery, that day's cashier, gave her a thumbs-up when Nick bent down to use his bank card. Leni shook

her head, letting her know there was nothing between them.

They left the shopping cart behind after pulling out the bags of groceries. The return trip to
her house was quick. In minutes, they had all of
Nick's supplies on the counter.

He washed his hands. "Meatballs first. Why
don't you go check on your mom while I work?"

She agreed, tiptoed down the hall, opened the
door a crack and saw her mom sleeping above
the covers on the four-poster bed.

In the kitchen again, she asked, "What can I
do to help?"

"I cook alone," he said, his hand up to the wrist
in the hamburger meat. She could see he'd added
onion and some breadcrumbs.

"Are those going to be good?"

"They're going to be fabulous."

She laughed. "Stop that!"

"Why?" He caught her gaze. "I like to hear
your laugh."

Her heart warmed, even though she told herself it wasn't supposed to. The smooth, sophisticated Nick was charming and almost irresistible
but shift to normal Nick and they were looking
at irresistible in the rearview mirror. She could
have melted at his feet.

And she couldn't do that. Even if she didn't
have a sick father and decisions to be made about

her biological father's estate, Nick did not have those kinds of feelings for her.

She walked around the center island of the kitchen to the sugar cookies her mom had abandoned. Taking note of how many there were, she went to the cabinet to get some containers.

"I used to make people laugh all the time."

His comment came out of nowhere and she leaned around to look at him. "Oh, yeah? I thought you said you weren't funny." She pulled two big containers and one small one from the cabinet and headed back to the island.

He glanced at the cookies, his eyes narrowing as if they confused him. But he said, "I wasn't funny, per se. All my life I'd been something of a daredevil. I bungee jumped before it was wise or popular."

She snorted, as she began stacking cookies in the containers.

"I did tricks on the Jet Ski."

"Like a dog?"

"No. Like a stuntman." He shook his head. "And the reason I was pretty good with the ladies was all about having a good time."

"You're sure it's not your money and good looks?"

"I never flaunted my family's wealth."

"You don't have to. Your clothes tell the story."

"Not when I'm wearing jeans and a hoodie."

"All right. I'll give you that."

They were quiet for a second before he said, "So, you think I'm good-looking?"

Oh, she *wasn't* going to give him *that* one. The man was vain enough. "You don't?"

He chuckled. "You're not one for straight answers today."

She snapped the lid on the final container of sugar cookies. "I'm not going to feed into your vanity."

He said nothing for a second, creating the last meatball and setting it on a tray to take to the stove and the frying pan.

"I guess there was a time when I was vain."

"You guess?"

"It never crossed my mind that being lucky, showing people a good time, having some looks—" he gave her the side-eye and she laughed "—made me vain."

"So, what happened?"

He didn't reply, busy with the frying pan for the meatballs. She would have thought it was a natural pause in the conversation because he was wrapped up in his creation for lunch—which was beginning to look more like dinner—except she remembered other things he'd said. Like he'd had a brother who'd followed him around. She didn't remember seeing anything about a brother in the articles she'd read online about Kourakis Money Management. But when they were skating, he'd mentioned him.

"Was your brother in on all this fun?"

"My brother died."

His words shocked her so much, she stopped dead in her tracks.

Remembering her feelings the day before, when she'd heard about her dad, seeing him sedated, hooked up to equipment that kept him alive, her chest hollowed out, helplessness and fear rose as strong and sharp as they had been in that minute. Nick had experienced all of that and more. His brother had *died*. Her dad was alive and strong. Whatever the doctors told him had to be done, her dad would fight to do it.

Nick's brother was gone.

She watched him roll the meatballs in the pan and place them on a tray to bake. His face wasn't solemn as it had been her first few days in New York, but now that she'd heard more of his past, she could see that he didn't have secrets as much as he held something of himself back.

Whether he was afraid of another loss or simply still tired from the grief, she didn't know. But she did know that asking him about his brother had changed him back into the guy who'd taken her to New York. The businesslike guy who didn't smile.

And maybe he needed a break?

"Tell me more about bungee jumping."

The expression on his face clearly said he knew she'd changed the subject and he was grateful. "It's exhilarating."

"You'd never get me to do something like that!"

"You think?" He laughed. "I never have a problem persuading people to do fun things."

Oh, she'd bet that was true. Gazing into his mischievous brown eyes, she saw the devilish guy who'd probably had his pick of adventures and his pick of women.

She sniffed a laugh. "You're such a con artist."

The last meatball on the tray and the tray in the oven, he faced her. "Not at all."

"Come on."

"I'm serious. I can tell when someone's genuinely afraid to bungee jump or skydive and I don't push."

"Right."

"I don't."

"And you never use that charm of yours on women?"

"I'm always honest. Especially with women."

When he looked at her like that, his dark eyes sincere and seductive, her chest pinched. Her breathing stuttered. Her eyes felt locked to his.

He'd been honest with her.

He put one hand on the counter beside her, so he could lean in, angling their faces inches from each other. "I don't have to be a con artist. Because I'm honest with women, they can be honest with me. Enjoy me while I enjoy them."

Oh...

The chest pinch tightened. She wasn't entirely sure she knew how to breathe.

"It always starts with a kiss…a light one… more like a brush to see if there are sparks."

Now for sure she couldn't breathe. Her entire body poised in anticipation of a kiss—the one she'd longed for—just one kiss to let her know she was more than a woman he'd babysat.

But he didn't move. Their eyes might be locked. He might have her trapped against the kitchen island, but he didn't move.

She stood frozen. Waiting. And feeling like an idiot for waiting. If he wanted to kiss her, he would.

But he didn't.

Just when she could have wiggled away from him, he bent his head and brushed his lips along hers. The sparks that flew could have set the kitchen on fire. Her nerves popped. The blood in her veins woke and exploded. Her lungs collapsed from lack of oxygen.

She expected him to pull away. After all, his demonstration was over. And she'd gotten her kiss. They could walk away now.

He did pull back a millimeter, but he paused. She opened her eyes to find herself inches away from his dark, dark gaze.

Nick knew he should pull back. God help him, he hadn't been able to resist shifting the conversation so far away from Joe that they'd never get back to it again, but the joke had been on him. The second his lips touched hers he knew he wanted more. He'd told himself that he could control any simple want but somehow that want became a need. Sharp and sensual, it wound through his blood, and after only five seconds of gazing into her eyes, he knew she felt it, too.

He leaned in again and took her mouth fully this time.

She put her hands on his cheeks and pushed off the counter, pressing herself against him. Need ricocheted through him. Her soft breasts met his chest, even as her hands kept him right where he was, as if she were afraid he would stop kissing her.

He wouldn't.

He yanked her tightly against him. He swore he could feel the frantic beating of her heart—

When that registered, he froze. He wasn't sure if her heart was beating that hard from excitement, or fear or the craziness of the whole thing, but whichever, it was wrong. She had a sick father and decisions to make about Mark Hinton's estate. She didn't need the likes of him seducing her, then dumping her. Because that's what he did. Moved on.

Leni was the kind of woman a man stayed with—

But he'd never stayed with a woman. Especially not a woman so sweet and sincere that he didn't deserve her.

He would hurt her.

He pulled away slowly, watched her eyes open and smiled at her. He could keep this uncomplicated. The past few years, he'd been a master at holding back his feelings, keeping things simple. He called on that gift.

"And that's just step one."

She licked her lips, held his gaze and whispered, "I'm not sure I'd survive step two."

Part of him yearned to believe he affected her as much as she affected him. To believe that kiss meant something. But he knew himself. He didn't make commitments. He couldn't. No woman should be saddled with a guy so riddled with guilt he buried himself in work.

Plus, like her, he wasn't sure *he'd* survive step two either. They had some powerful chemistry. But all that would do is lure her in and make it hurt worse when he left her.

He eased back, away from her. "Luckily, we don't have to worry about that."

"Yeah. Lucky." She pulled her hand through her shiny hair. "How much longer for the meatballs?"

"I usually give them a half hour."

"Okay."

She looked as confused and befuddled as he felt. They both needed a break. Leaning against the stove, he said, "Why don't you take a nap, too?"

"No. I'm fine."

"I know you are. But I have a few calls I'd like to make while I wait for the meatballs."

The relief on her face would have killed his ego if he hadn't known how much she'd enjoyed that kiss. "Maybe a rest is a good idea."

"We all want you and your mom sharp when you speak to the neurologist."

She pulled her hand through her hair one more time. "Yeah."

"Go."

She nodded and scrambled out of the kitchen.

Nick let his head fall. Holy hell. That kiss tempted him to do things that would only hurt Leni. Tempted him to believe in something he wasn't even sure he understood. When he looked at himself, his life, his regrets, he knew he had to stay away. But, oh, how he wanted her. Just one night.

If he thought he could take one night without hurting her, he would. But he couldn't. He'd seen so many glimpses into her heart that he knew how soft she was. Vulnerable, though she hid it with humor.

He had to get away and stay away.

CHAPTER TEN

LENI'S MOM WOKE about three o'clock. The meatballs were out of the oven and had been marinating in sauce. Nick put the spaghetti in a pot while Leni brought the salad out of the fridge and set the table.

When they sat down to eat, Denise said, "This is nice."

Glad her mom looked awake and normal, Leni reached for the salad bowl. "Did you have a good rest, Mom?"

"Yes." She laughed. "I must have needed it. If you don't mind, after we eat, I'd like to get a shower and go directly to the hospital."

Nick said, "Whatever you want."

Leni winced. "I'm sorry—" She carefully peeked at Nick. They hadn't really made eye contact since that kiss, but she knew why. The touch of their lips had been electric. Something neither one of them had expected. That led to the bigger kiss, the better kiss, the *real* kiss. It was a demonstration gone off the rails and they both knew it. "—I never gave you the chance to shower."

"I didn't bring anything to change into. I had to race to my jet to beat you to Topeka." He laughed. "I'm getting accustomed to wearing the same clothes for two days when I'm around you."

Denise looked horrified. "She's not trouble, is she?"

"No. She's very easy to get along with."

Leni's heart stumbled. Nick wouldn't look at her when he said it, but his ears got red.

He liked her.

He'd said it before, a couple different ways. And that kiss more or less proved it. But they'd only known each other six days. If she wasn't an heir, she'd be returning to Mannington, never to see Nick Kourakis again.

She'd gotten her kiss. The one kiss she wanted. She should be content with that.

Except—

Nobody had ever kissed her like that, and she was about damned certain no one ever would again. It seemed wrong, absolutely positively wrong, to walk away without at least exploring that.

But he didn't want to. He'd warned her off. Still, he'd warned her off before they'd gotten to know each other. Now that she'd had a few glimpses into his life, she was willing to guess that his aloofness had something to do with the loss of his brother.

What if she could help him through that?

What if fate had brought them together because whatever they felt, it was strong enough to ease him out of his mourning and back to life again?

It was risky.

But she couldn't leave him stranded in the limbo he seemed to live. She'd seen him sullen and quiet in New York and happy here in Mannington. There was a connection. She knew it.

The question was, did she want to risk rejection and heartbreak for a man she'd known six days?

They finished eating. Denise left the kitchen to shower. When she was ready to go, they climbed into Nick's SUV and headed for the hospital.

It was dark when they reached it. The moon rose over the buildings and the trees around it. Christmas decorations at nurses' stations, over doorways and in windows went unnoticed as they walked through the corridors to the ICU.

They waited an hour for the doctor, but Leni gratefully used the time to tease her dad and watch her mom relax degree by degree the more her dad teased and chatted.

The neurologist arrived with two younger men, one of them rolling a cart with a computer. He explained that there was scarring in her dad's brain, in a very good place. Which sounded like an oxymoron until he said, "It's a good place because we can remove it."

Her mom's eyes widened. "You're saying brain surgery?"

"Yes. And as with any surgery there are risks, especially when we enter the brain. But we're confident that once the scarring that's been building since his injury is removed, his seizures will disappear."

They asked the neurologist a million questions. Nick leaned against the windowsill, listening, adding a comment or question here and there.

Leni took it all in. But in the end, she felt the surgery had too much promise to ignore.

Except she wouldn't want it done in Kansas unless the best neurosurgeon in the world worked there. To hire the best neurosurgeon in the world, she'd need money.

And she might have money. Tons of it. If Mark Hinton was her biological dad.

The weirdness of it almost did her in. She wouldn't have the wonderful father she had now if her biological father had wanted her. But he hadn't wanted her, so she didn't want him either. Except she needed him to save the father she wouldn't have had if he hadn't abandoned her. The logic scrambled her brain.

They stayed with her dad after the neurologist left, discussing pros and cons, but when visiting hours were over, they went home.

Exhausted, talked out, Denise went to her room. Nick faced Leni. "Are you okay?"

"Yeah, I'm fine. I just have a lot of thinking to do and need time on the computer researching everything that doctor said."

Nick laughed. "You like to research."

"Smart people do." She took a breath. "I'm going to be looking for the best neurosurgeon on the planet. Someone who's done this surgery hundreds of times."

"Makes sense."

She caught Nick's gaze. "To employ him, I'm going to need tons of money."

He studied her for a second. "You need your inheritance."

"Yes."

"You don't seem very happy about it."

She sucked in a breath. "It's weird. To help the father who raised me, I have to accept the help of the man who abandoned me."

"Did you ever stop to think that this would be what Mark would want to do?"

She sniffed a laugh. "What?"

"Mark wasn't a bad guy. He was an overworked, very paranoid, fearful guy. He didn't abandon you as much as he counted on your mom to take care of you. I'll bet he hadn't even known your mother was in trouble."

"He never checked on us."

"He barely got himself to work some days. The only time he was happy and felt safe was fishing in the middle of the ocean. Hundreds of thousands of people depended on him for jobs. He knew the pressure of that."

"So much that he didn't have time for one little girl."

"Don't think of it like that. Think of the stress, the pressure."

She pressed her lips together.

"Leni, your father had very few happy days. You love life. I'll bet after your experience in foster care, it wasn't easy for you to get to that place emotionally. But the Longs helped you. They made you the person you are today. Don't throw away your happiness over this. Take a deep breath, be glad for the money to save your father and forgive Mark. Otherwise this will ruin your life."

There was so much wisdom in what Nick said that she let it sink in. Especially since she almost felt herself forgiving Mark Hinton for abandoning her. Not only had his stepping aside resulted in her having the best parents in the world, but also his gift of money would save her dad. How could she stay angry with him after that?

A strange warmth filled her soul, a lightness, as if she'd done the right thing.

"I get it."

"It's difficult that your dad has to have the surgery, but I don't think you'll be sorry you're opting into the estate."

"I hope you're right."

"I am. Don't use my screwed-up life to judge what it's like to be wealthy. I had everything at my disposal as a child and I had choices about things like where I went to school, joining the Navy, even jet-setting after leaving the SEALs. I had the most amazing life."

"That's true."

"Had it not been for my brother dying, my life would have stayed very, very good and I'd probably be on a beach somewhere now."

She searched his eyes. He was telling her everything would turn out okay and she appreciated that. But there was more, a bigger story in his eyes, sadness over his brother's death. She simply didn't know how to get to it. Or even if she should try.

"You wouldn't have come home for Christmas?"

"I would have been home Christmas morning. I always made it in time for gift exchange with my family. But the big picture is I had a life I loved. I worked, just not in a conventional way. I wouldn't have been stuck in my office all day or doing Danny's bidding when he couldn't get out of a trial."

"Then you wouldn't have met me."

He looked away. "Yes, and how blissful it would have been not to know that I was a vain guy who lied to his parents."

She laughed. Every time the conversation became about him, he deflected. But she understood that. It was part of why she couldn't get to his sadness. He didn't want her to.

Before she could say anything, he pushed away from the counter. "Anyhow, if you don't need me, I'm going to leave you to your research. I've got some work I have to do, too."

"Okay. Give me a second to fix up the guest room."

He caught her arm as she turned to scamper away. "I said that wrong. I'm going back to the airport to hop in my jet, and work through the flight home."

"Oh."

Her brain stalled. Why would he want to leave? It was late. He was clearly tired. He shouldn't drive an hour to an airstrip and spend even more hours in the air before he got home. Of course, he did have a bedroom in his jet. And he'd given a week of his busy life to entertain her. He really could be behind in his work.

She opted to stay positive. He was a busy guy. He had to get back to his job. The man had kissed her like a guy so smitten he couldn't help himself. And he'd taken the time to help her see she needed to forgive Mark Hinton. Whatever was between them, it was growing.

His leaving had nothing to do with her and she would respect his choice.

"I can't thank you enough for your help."

"It was my pleasure. But it's time for me to get home."

"Okay. Sounds good."

Within minutes he was leaving, outside her parents' house, ready to climb into his rented SUV. She stood beside the vehicle door, handing him a plastic container of homemade Christmas cookies, not quite sure what to say or do.

In her heart of hearts, she hoped he'd catch her shoulders and lean down to kiss her goodbye. No preliminary kidding around this time. She wanted the invitation kiss. The one that said *I like you. There might be something here worth exploring.*

She wanted *that* kiss.

But he didn't catch her shoulders and lean in to touch his lips to hers. He looked at the container of cookies with the weirdest expression, as if no one had ever done anything nice for him, his lips kicking into a crooked smile.

"Are these the iced sugar cookies I saw on the counter?"

She stuffed her cold hands into the pockets of her old coat. "Yep."

"They looked wonderful."

"I saw you eyeing them."

He shook his head. "You don't miss anything."

She said, "No. I don't," hoping he realized she was telling him that she knew what was going on between them wasn't simple or easy. She was a small-town girl with the most basic of educations. He'd traveled the world, served in the military, had been raised in luxury. It probably wasn't wise for them to start a romance.

But after that kiss, how could they not?

He opened the SUV door, tucked the cookies on the passenger seat and turned to her.

"I probably won't see you until after Danny gets the DNA results."

Hope tingled through her. He could have easily gotten into the vehicle when he put the cookies inside. Instead here he was, only a few inches away from her. Close enough to touch. Close enough for him to kiss her.

"I need to be here anyway."

"Okay." He paused a few seconds, gave her a weak smile, then slid behind the steering wheel. "See you in a couple of days."

He wasn't going to kiss her. He wasn't going to go in for seconds, after that amazing kiss?

He'd said the kiss had been a demonstration, and the first part might have been. But the second part had been real. She *knew* it.

She took a step back. "Yeah. See you then."

He closed the door and drove off. She stood shivering in the driveway, watching his taillights disappear in the darkness, vibrating with feelings she didn't understand. It had been the best two days and the worst two days. She'd forgiven her biological father because like it or not, his money would save her adoptive father. A father she loved.

But something else had happened. With that kiss, Nick admitted that he liked her, and driving away as he had, he'd admitted he wasn't going to do anything about it.

Rejection spiked. Sharp, miserable, edged with darkness.

She closed her eyes, telling herself not to be foolish. Today was Saturday. She'd met Nick the Monday before. They'd only known each other six days. She was foolish to be upset or even concerned that he hadn't kissed her again.

She took a breath, fighting the feeling of not being good enough, knowing why her mind had gone in that direction. She might have forgiven Mark Hinton for not wanting her, but that didn't mean her biological parents' rejections hadn't left a mark.

She needed to get over that, too. But a sense of unworthiness ran deep, and she had no idea how to let it go. Wash it away. Send it off into the universe.

But she would figure it out. She had to. She'd accepted her dad's money. She'd felt that lightness in her soul. Moving on was the right thing to do.

Now she just had to figure out how.

Her father came home from the hospital the next morning. He'd gotten some new meds and appeared to be totally back to being himself. After twenty-four hours of Leni and her mother watching him like two hawks, she'd returned to work at the diner. She *might* be inheriting tons of money, but they didn't have it now and they had bills to pay. And there was also the chance she wasn't an heir. Everyone was so sure Mark Hinton was her father. She had niggling doubts.

After the lunch rush and before the dinner rush, George went to the back steps to smoke and Leni found herself alone in the diner again. As she had been the day Nick arrived.

Longing swept through her. She let herself feel it but didn't get carried away. The confusion and emotions of potentially inheriting billions of dollars and her dad's illness could have made her crazy. She knew to control her feelings, her reactions. She'd done it before, when in foster care. She'd call on that discipline again.

The pocket of her apron buzzed, and she pulled out her cell phone. Seeing Waters, Waters and Montgomery in the caller ID, she had to sit.

This was it.

"Hello, Danny."

"And hello to you, Miss Leni Long…confirmed child of Mark Hinton."

Her breathing stopped. "Mark Hinton really was my dad?"

"Three DNA samples don't lie."

"Oh, my gosh." The truth of it rattled through

her, not finding footing because she wasn't sure what it all meant. How her life would change. But Danny was right. DNA didn't lie. And though she hadn't been a hundred percent certain she wanted Mark Hinton to be her dad, she had made her peace with that, too.

Something *Nick* had encouraged *her* to do.

She told herself to stop thinking about him. They were good together. Sort of. At least she thought so. But right now, she had more important things to figure out.

Danny's voice brought her back to the present. "So, I'll need you in New York again to run through a few things. The estate can't be distributed until all the heirs are found, but with this proof you have access to your share of the money."

Meaning, she could get her dad the best neurosurgeon in the world.

Her heart sped up. That was her priority.

"When do you want me?"

"Tomorrow?"

"So, I'd fly out today?"

"Or I can arrange for Nick to come and get you."

No. The time for depending on Nick was over. She wanted to be smart Leni. The foster child who'd adapted to her surroundings, studied, put herself through university. So, he could stop thinking of her as a responsibility and start seeing her as…a friend, for now. The other stuff, the romantic stuff, would blossom if it was meant to be. But she wouldn't push or even think about it. It was time to put her best foot forward.

"I can fly commercial." She laughed. "Actually, I'll make my own reservations."

Danny said, "Okay. The estate will reimburse you. Since you wouldn't get here until this evening flying today, make the arrangements for early tomorrow morning and reservations at the hotel where you'd been staying. When you get to New York, you can come right to the office and we can get down to business."

"Thanks."

"You're welcome. And, Leni." He paused. "Congratulations. Your life is about to change in the best possible ways."

She said, "Thanks," but the doubts she'd been fighting all along flooded her brain again. She was a blue-collar woman entering a diamond-necklace world. And maybe that was another thing she needed to change? Nick only knew her as needy Leni. In her worn coat and scruffy jeans. With the sick dad.

But she wasn't needy anymore. She had billions of dollars at her disposal. She could start looking for a neurosurgeon and maybe get some new clothes, so she didn't always feel out of place.

It was time to step into her new life.

When they disconnected the call, she searched

online for her hotel, called the number and made reservations. When that part of the call was complete, she asked for the concierge and within seconds he said, "Can I help you?"

"Yes. You probably don't remember me, but I stayed at your hotel last week." She winced at how stupid she sounded and pulled in a breath. "I'm going to be there again this week. Nick Kourakis told me that if I needed anything or needed to *find* anything in New York, you were the one to ask."

"Absolutely. How can I assist you?"

"I need some clothes. Really *nice* clothes. Good clothes. Clothes that scream *money*."

He laughed and gave her the names of three shops near the hotel, eased her fears about looking like a grandma when one of them was the boutique Nick had suggested, and wished her a good day.

She immediately looked up the three stores and smiled. He really did know his job. All three offered private consultations and Leni made appointments for the following afternoon. She wasn't going to play this by ear. Her life was changing, and she couldn't pretend it wasn't.

She would more than step into her world. She would take control.

CHAPTER ELEVEN

LENI HAD BOOKED the earliest morning flight, but with the time difference she arrived in New York City after eleven o'clock. She got to Danny's building around noon, and she had her appointment at the first shop at two. She didn't have to rush.

She accepted the three no-limit credit cards Danny gave her and the checkbook with accompanying bank card. He explained there were three heirs, but there was wording in the will that might result in her only getting one quarter rather than one third of her dad's estate—still, billions of dollars.

She told him she couldn't understand why anybody would fight about that and Danny had laughed. Then he slid into a conversation about security. She would be getting a limo with a driver.

That part concerned her, but she kept it to herself. She was an heir now. There would be plenty of things about this life that would be different.

She had decided not merely to accept that but to take control. Today was the day all that started.

With her briefing complete, she took off for her appointments at the stores. Her new driver—parked at the building entrance and waiting for her—drove to the address Leni gave him, a small shop on an out-of-the-way street.

She pushed open the etched-glass door and walked into a sea of merchandise showcased in a room with black woodwork, white walls, upside-down fishbowl light fixtures and bronze tin ceilings.

Leni held back a *Wow*.

"Can I help you?"

"Yes. I have an appointment at two."

The clerk smiled and pointed to a set of steps that had been painted black. "Upstairs. Third floor. With Iris."

On her way to find Iris, she noticed the first floor was filled with bohemian clothes. Things she could see herself wearing in her downtime. The second floor was filled with what she considered work clothes. Pants, soft sweaters, pencil skirts, shiny blouses and dresses. All of them beautiful.

She didn't see a person until she reached the top of the third flight of stairs. Two women and a man stood in a semicircle in front of three full-length mirrors. Except for two chairs near the mirrors, the room was empty.

"Elenore?" Dressed in a black sheath and pearls, the older woman walked over and took her hands before kissing both of her cheeks.

"You must be Iris." Leni pulled back, ignoring the cheek kisses which she thought a bit much, and examining the black sheath and pearls. Lovely and obviously expensive, but not quite the image she wanted to project.

"It's such a pleasure to have you at our store."

Okay. She knew the woman had no idea she was one of the Hinton heirs but apparently making an appointment came with certain assumptions. "I'm glad to be here."

"What are you looking for?" Iris asked. "Casual, business or formal?"

Leni said, "All of them."

Iris smiled and faced the young man and thirty-something woman in jeans standing next to her. "Bill, Mandy, let's start with casual clothes and work our way to formal."

When Iris and her team left, Leni glanced around the room. Though another person might consider a shopping trip oodles of fun, she was on a mission. She had to look like she belonged in her new world. And, yeah, buying a ton of clothes probably was going to be fun.

A few minutes later, Iris and her employees each brought an armload of jeans, shirts and sweaters. Leni instantly fell in love with a white silk blouse and pumpkin-colored wool pants, a green sweater and artificially aged jeans, with high-heel ankle booties. Still, not everything they brought was her style, so she went out to the floor and waded through racks of jeans and pants, dresses, skirts and blouses and matching jewelry.

That's when the joy of it hit her. She could have anything she wanted. It was both exciting and humbling, and in some ways confusing.

But Iris was always beside her, talking about fit and tailoring. Bill and Mandy went ahead of her, pulling things they recommended. Now that they had seen a bit of her taste in clothes, Bill had an eye for casual wear that screamed big money while still being comfortable and Mandy knew the colors Leni looked best in.

Just when she thought she was done and wouldn't even have to go to the other two stores, Iris said, "Now, let's talk formal wear."

"I don't plan on going anywhere formal."

Iris chuckled. "This is New York City, darling. You won't be going out to dinner on a Friday in anything less than a cocktail dress. And if you're staying through the holiday, you'll also be going to a Christmas ball or two."

Mandy scrambled over, carrying two gowns. One green velvet, which Leni knew would make her eyes look amazing. The other a red flowing thing that caused Leni's heart to chug to a stop. Bill brought an armload of shorter dresses, half of which sparkled.

She remembered Nick's mom mentioning a Christmas ball and a Christmas party at the children's ward for the hospital. She'd said she'd attend, so if she got an official invitation, she intended to be ready.

She tried on the shorter dresses and the green velvet, saving the red one for last. Everything worked. The soft, supple fabrics cruised along her skin like a lover's caress. Bill and Mandy pinned the waistlines of three of the cocktail dresses to perfect their fit.

Iris stood on the sidelines approving everything.

When they were done and Leni was back in her old jeans and worn T-shirt, she handed Iris one of the no-limit credit cards.

Though Leni waited nervously, the card was approved in seconds. Iris returned it to her, and she glanced at it. It didn't look any different than her own Mastercard, but it worked a hundred times better.

Walking to her limo, she cancelled her other two appointments and had her driver take her to the hotel where she'd reserved a suite, the same one where she'd stayed on her last trip. Less than an hour later, her purchases began arriving with bellboy after bellboy rolling carts of bags and boxes into her room.

She wanted to laugh—who wouldn't?—but the reality of having so much stuff stopped her cold.

First off, she thought about buying luggage, so she could take it all home—then she realized she probably wouldn't wear a lot of these clothes in Mannington. Maybe the jeans. And the really cute boots. But most of this "stuff" she would wear in only New York. Danny had mentioned her serving on the board of one or more of her dad's companies and she liked the idea.

Really liked it.

She would see firsthand how businesses were run, have a part in the decision making, make sure employees were paid decently and no one harassed an injured employee the way her dad had been harassed.

She felt the reality of her new life clicking in. She wasn't just a woman who was getting billions of dollars. She had responsibilities. Choices. Options. Power.

And she'd probably have to be in New York as much as she was in Mannington. So maybe she needed to get a condo? She couldn't move all these fabulous clothes to and from Mannington. It simply made more sense to have a home here. She'd spent her teen years thinking she'd be a social worker in Topeka, but with the newly inherited fortune, she could see herself doing so much more for her community.

That's when she knew she needed to sit, breathe. She called room service for tea and curled up on the red sofa, letting everything sink in, going over her quick decisions, making sure she wasn't reacting when she should be planning.

Feeling out of sorts, Nick left work early. Today had been the day when Leni met with Danny to discuss specifics. He told himself he didn't care. He told himself the Hinton money wasn't any of his business until the estate was settled and the time came to discuss where the heirs would put their money.

Entering his condo, he ignored the silence that greeted him, but after having been with chatty Leni for days, through some tough things, but also some fun things like skating and the Irish pub, the quiet of his home was deafening.

He tossed his briefcase to the sofa. But as he turned, he saw the little plastic container of cookies on his dining room table.

Christmas cookies. Homemade. Not cookies his mom had ordered from the exclusive bakery in Long Island. Not cookies made by her friend who'd studied pastry in Paris.

Just plain, iced sugar cookies with sprinkles.

He walked over, opened the container and took a cookie. He bit into it and the soft, buttery confection melted in his mouth.

He groaned. He couldn't remember ever eating a cookie this good. He also couldn't remember the last time anybody had done something so simple, so thoughtful. Six cookies in a little plastic container had almost done him in. As she'd put it into his hand, he'd nearly melted.

He'd nearly kissed her again.

Which was wrong.

He shook his head, went into his bedroom to change into jeans and went to his kitchen to order takeout—

But he remembered that Leni had been through a difficult weekend with her dad in the hospital. Monday, Danny had called and told her she was an heir. This morning she'd flown to New York and had a meeting with Danny.

Her head was probably spinning.

He'd bet it was.

And she had no one in New York to talk to.

Concern for her filled him. But as much as he wanted to help her, he couldn't really ask her to dinner. That was too date like.

He looked at the cookies. So full of Christmas cheer. The spirit of it filled him. Peace on earth. Being kind to each other. Helping each other—

He slid his phone from his jeans pocket. He hit her number in the contacts section and within seconds her phone was ringing.

"Hey."

Sounding totally surprised, she said, "Hey. What's up?"

"I know you had a busy day with Danny but—" Feeling like a sixteen-year-old asking for a date, he had to remind himself that he was calling for her. He wanted to hear how her dad was, but he also knew she was probably overwhelmed about the estate and would need to talk. If he had to stretch a truth to find a way to give her that time, so be it.

"I was thinking about going Christmas shopping tonight. For my mom," he clarified, to make the story work. "Since you made fun of the boutique, I thought maybe you'd like to come with me and help me find a more hip store."

"I'd love to."

"Good. I'll be at your hotel in ten minutes. Is that enough time?"

"Sure."

"And then maybe we could get a bite."

"Okay."

"Okay. My limo will be outside your hotel in ten."

He hung up feeling better. Infinitely better. But only because he liked her enough that he wanted to be sure she was okay. Not because it was a date, or anything close. He just wanted to be sure she had someone to talk to.

Leni disconnected the call and stared at the phone, but only for a few seconds. Nick's offer might have confused her but she didn't have time to wonder if this was a date. She had to change into one of her new pairs of jeans, a cashmere sweater and the hottest-of-hot black leather jacket.

Riding down the elevator to the lobby, she told herself this wasn't anything special. He needed help shopping and, after today, she felt like a shopping pro. She was a perfect choice to help him.

It was all good.

She stepped out of the lobby onto the street and into the falling snow. Though Nick stood by the door of his limo, she tipped her face up, let herself enjoy the soft wet snow and Christmas spirit that shuffled through the air around her. Christmas in New York City might feel different than at home—shinier and more expensive—but it was still Christmas.

As she reached the door, she said, "Hey! Thanks for asking me to help you shop. The hotel really was starting to close in on me."

"You're welcome." He winced. "But I had an ulterior motive. And more than help with finding my mom a Christmas gift. I wanted to hear about your dad."

She slid into the limo and Nick followed her. "He's fine. Really good. New meds are keeping everything stable, but after a few hours of hunting for the world's best neurosurgeon, I realized I was out of my league and contacted his neurologist. He and I are now on a quest for the best neurosurgeon on the planet."

Nick sighed. "That's really good."

"It is. So, what are you thinking about getting your mom?"

He shook his head. "No idea. I just know that you dissing my favorite shop sent a shot of panic through me. If my mother hasn't liked my gifts all these years, I've failed."

She laughed as the limo pulled out into traffic. "Failed?"

"My brother used to buy the best gifts."

Her heart stilled at his mention of his brother, but she casually said, "Oh, yeah?"

"Yes. He'd find the cashmere sweater in that year's 'hot' color, when I didn't even know years had hot colors."

"Oh, they do. One year it's pink. The next year it's olive."

He peeked at her. "And you know this?"

"Of course, I know this. I might not live in New York, but I don't live under a rock." She pulled out her phone, searched *hot color*. "And speaking of living under rocks. I'm thinking I might need a place in New York."

His eyebrows rose. "Really."

"Yeah. I bought a bunch of clothes today." She stopped long enough to roll her eyes. "I mean a *bunch*. And I realized I wouldn't wear half of them in Mannington, and would only need them for board meetings for Mark Hinton's..." She paused and amended that to, "my dad's companies."

Nick heard the change in her voice. She really had begun to accept that Mark Hinton was her dad.

When he said, "I'm glad," he wasn't just talking about being glad that she'd be attending board meetings. He was glad she seemed to be adjusting to who she really was.

He'd also noticed the black leather jacket, the trendy jeans, the new boots and her own cashmere sweater. "You look good."

She looked *great*. She looked like someone stepping into her future, becoming herself.

"Thanks. Anyway, when I realized I shouldn't lug all this stuff to Mannington where I probably wouldn't wear it anyway, I thought about getting my own place."

She truly was moving into her role. Nick couldn't have been any prouder and he knew Mark would have been, too.

"I think it's a good idea."

"Yes. I'm sure Mark had a condo here, but Danny reminded me we don't want to use my dad's condos or houses or jets and alert the media that I've been found, so I thought, hey, I have billions of dollars at my disposal. I don't need to stay in a hotel."

He smiled, warmth filling him. She was so cute and so smart. "No. You don't."

"So, tomorrow I may call a real estate agent and start looking."

"I know a person or two. I could make a call. I'll tell them you are a friend from the Midwest and ask for discretion."

She peeked over at him. "And you'll get it?"

Making eye contact took the warmth that always filled him when she was around and turned it to the kind of heat that would be nothing but trouble for them. So, he glanced away. "The price you'll pay for a condo will result in a hefty commission. Remember how I told you about not kissing and telling?"

She nodded, but her face turned red. Reminding her of the kiss had been a bad idea. Not just for her. She might be embarrassed but the heat already in his system turned to molten lava.

He sucked in a quiet breath, hoping she didn't notice. "Well, it works the same for real estate agents. Wealthy people need discretion. Real estate agents provide it to get their return business. And their friends' business. Discretion is like currency to them."

She nodded and pulled her phone from her jacket pocket. "I got my things today from this great boutique. And they had a top that I'm positive your mother would like." She hit her screen a few times, then displayed the address.

Glad she got both their minds off that kiss, Nick texted it to his driver and in five minutes they were standing in front of the etched-glass door.

Snow fell around them. Leni's face glowed in the light of a streetlamp as they walked to the door. "I might get something for my mom, too."

"I thought you said this wasn't a mom store."

"It isn't." She led the way to the door. "My mom's very youthful. Your mom's a trendsetter."

He laughed, especially when he realized there was a difference. Leni really was rubbing off on him.

They walked into the shop and Nick noticed Christmas music playing softly in the background. Tinsel edged the front counter. A ring of poinsettias almost hid the cash register.

"Leni! You're back!"

"Here to Christmas shop, Mandy," Leni happily said.

Nick wasn't surprised Leni remembered the clerk's name or that the clerk remembered Leni's. She'd probably spent a hundred thousand dollars that afternoon.

"Looking for a sweater for my mom and something like a kimono for his."

Nick frowned. "Kimono?"

"Something long and luxurious. Almost a duster," Leni clarified, talking to the clerk. "I want her to be able to wear it with jeans when she's shopping and look like queen of the world."

An older woman came down the stairs talking. "I have just the thing."

"Hey, Iris!"

"Hey, Leni. Who's your friend?"

"Nick. His mom is New York high society. I

want to put her in an outfit that will make her feel funky and cool."

Iris laughed. "For when she lunches with her friends, so she looks like the hip one?"

"Exactly."

Nick had no idea what a kimono was, but apparently it was a good choice because Leni didn't merely gasp when Iris led them to one in the back, she touched it reverently.

"Silk," Iris said.

"It's perfect."

Nick studied it. Pale blue like his mom's eyes, it didn't look like something she might wear, but it did look like something Joe would have bought her.

"I like it," he ventured uncertainly.

Iris said, "Are you sure?"

"I've just never bought my mother something that I haven't already seen her in."

"You mean something similar?" Leni said.

"Yes."

Sliding her hand beneath his arm and nestling against him, she laughed. "Well, she will love this."

After a quick squeeze, Leni headed for three rows of sweaters and chose four for her mother. Nick stood behind her, not quite uncomfortable because shopping with a purpose almost felt okay.

Actually, watching Leni ponder sweaters for her mom gave him a boost. He knew Denise would love them, but he also knew her mom needed them. Seeing the joy on Leni's face at being able to buy things for her mother filled him with that indescribable feeling again. The feeling he had when she savored the wine. The feeling he had when she gave him Christmas cookies.

When they stepped out into the street, into falling snow with Christmas lights and tinsel billowing in the wind, he recognized it. This was the feeling he'd had as a child, the breathless wish for a toy or a video game he wasn't even sure his parents knew existed, the childish wonder of a holiday made for parties and presents. A day his dad didn't work or talk about work. His mom beamed over roast turkey and pie. And he and his brother couldn't sleep for anticipation.

And he didn't want to lose it.

He wanted this feeling to last forever.

If Leni was the reason why he felt it, he wasn't letting her go yet.

"How about another trip to the Irish pub?"

Her eyes widened. "Absolutely."

He opened the limo door for her and she slid inside. In a few minutes, they were climbing out again and heading for the little bar.

Celtic Christmas music poured out as he yanked on the door to let her enter first. In the few days that had passed, the place had been decked out with lights and tinsel.

"Now it really looks like the bar back home."

He laughed as the hostess said, "Good evening."

"Good evening. There are just two of us."

She smiled. "Right this way."

They walked back to the same table they'd had the last time they were there, and Nick wondered if it was a coincidence or if she remembered them.

He didn't say anything as they sat, but he recalled that day after skating. How much fun they'd had. How Leni had cuddled against him in the cold on the walk back to her hotel.

Feelings buffeted him, nudging him to take some time to think this through, but he ignored them in favor of keeping the wonderful mood they'd created.

He made her laugh over hamburgers and fries and encouraged her to have a third draft when she would have stopped at two.

"Today's the day your world changed. In a way, we're celebrating."

"I certainly spent enough money."

He smiled. "And you don't even have to care." He called for the waitress to bring the check. He gave her a credit card and she returned it with the receipt.

After he'd signed, he and Leni rose and slid into their coats. But out on the street, when his limo driver opened their door, he hesitated.

"Feel like walking?"

Her head tilted and she smiled, as if she remembered the last time they'd made this walk. "Yeah." She tucked her arm under his as he signaled for the driver that they would be walking.

Their feet made imprints in the snow that had fallen while they ate. Cold air filled his nostrils and horns beeped around them, but somehow it added to the magic. Everyone seemed to be laughing and chatting, carrying packages, talking about holiday plans.

Two blocks never went by so quickly.

They stomped the snow off their shoes and entered the lobby of her hotel. Though he considered letting her walk to her room herself, he got a weird, uncomfortable feeling about the day.

She, Danny, Mary Catherine, Jace and Nick himself should be the only five people who knew she was an heir. But administrative assistants and clerks saw papers all the time. People passing office doors heard things they shouldn't.

Leni was a small, soft, big-eyed girl from the Midwest, and though he was sure she could care for herself in normal situations, nothing about this situation was normal.

He motioned to the elevator and she headed there. An older couple joined them on the ride to her floor, so they didn't say anything. But as they ambled to her suite door, he remembered walking into the diner the first time he'd seen her. The elf suit. Their small talk. That wash of instant connection.

If he let himself, he could drift back to those few minutes. He could see her smile. He could feel his heart tumble when their eyes met.

Need spiked, sharp and sweet, along with something simple and reverent. He had never felt like that. And the pull of it was so strong his fingers tingled with the need to touch her, to tell her he was crazy about her—

But that wasn't right. She was on the brink of a whole new life. And even if she wasn't, she deserved so much more than him. Somebody so much better. Somebody special.

Still, he didn't even try to stop himself when instinct had him bending to brush his lips across hers. Quickly. Just a taste. He couldn't have her, but one little goodnight kiss didn't hurt.

She blinked at him.

He could almost hear her saying *Wow*, even though she didn't utter a word. He saw the intensity in her eyes and wished for thirty seconds he was a better man.

But he wasn't.

He knew who he was.

Not a liar. Not really a con man. Just somebody with the gift of persuasion. He could kiss her a million times, maybe even get her into bed. He could give her the best Christmas she'd ever had.

And then what?

What happened when she discovered he was responsible for his brother's death? That he wasn't lily white or even dingy gray? His soul was black from narcissism and selfishness that had led to losing his best friend.

Then what?

He'd become who he was: a solitary, stoic workaholic because he didn't want to hurt anybody else, but he also didn't care to feel the pain of that kind of rejection.

He would not take that risk.

CHAPTER TWELVE

LENI WAS ON her way to Danny's office the next morning to talk about when and how she'd get on the boards of some of her dad's companies, when her phone buzzed. Looking at the caller ID, she saw Nick's name and her heart perked up. He'd kissed her again the night before. Not the deep, romantic kiss he'd given her in her mother's kitchen. But a nice, normal goodnight kiss.

In some ways, that one had been more powerful. Filled with the happiness of their evening together, that kiss and been exactly what it should have been. Soft and sweet.

Still, she wasn't going to be a lovesick puppy about this. She would be cool and sophisticated. She answered her phone with a very casual, "Hey, Nick."

"Hey. I got a call from my mom this morning. She reminded me about the party in the children's ward that was supposed to be Friday afternoon. It's been moved up to tomorrow because we're in for a blizzard on Friday. I know it's short notice, but she'd love for you to be there."

She'd love, not *he'd* love.

She closed her eyes, telling herself it was idiotic to make that kind of distinction. The point was, they were getting more time together. More time to get to know each other. More time to figure out what was happening between them.

Striving to sound normal, she said, "Okay. I can be there. I only have a meeting with Danny, then my afternoon is free."

"Have your driver bring you to the hospital around one-thirty. Party starts at two o'clock, but if you get there a little early, I can show you around."

Her pulse kicked up. Just as he'd told her to come outside to his limo the day before, didn't come up to her hotel room to pick her up, he wasn't going to fetch her for the party either.

As if he were deliberately making the distinction that this wasn't a date.

She stopped that thought, too. They'd never get anywhere if she was so picky about everything. For all she knew, this was how dates happened in New York. Or maybe among rich people. Because everybody had a limo, nobody had to fetch anybody.

"Okay."

"Okay."

She hung up the phone, shaking her head, reminding herself she couldn't nitpick Nick's behavior. She had to roll with at least some things.

With the fundraiser only a day away, she could have gone shopping. But that seemed weird when she'd spent oodles of money the day before. Surely something in the eight tons of clothes she'd bought would be good enough.

In her suite, after her meeting with Danny, she looked up more information about the fundraiser and tons of articles popped onto her screen. She was only interested in seeing how people dressed, but then she saw a picture taken six years before—further back than she'd gone in her search of Kourakis Money Management the day she'd met Nick. The photo was of Nick and his parents and another man. The caption gave their names and the other man was Joe Kourakis.

His brother.

She stared at the picture. Nick looked like a kid. A bad kid. The kind of kid who stole cars for fun and broke the hearts of starry-eyed socialites. His brother didn't look old enough to be out of high school, but he was listed as CEO of Kourakis Money Management. Their mom's head was tilted back as she laughed. Even their dad was smiling.

She squeezed her eyes shut, thinking about how that little family had changed, reminded again that something about Nick's brother's death haunted him.

The temptation rose to ask him about his brother when she saw him the next day, but she couldn't bring up something so emotional at a public event and she also thought it wasn't right to ask. Nick should tell her. She should let him broach the subject.

Forcing her mind off that, she reminded herself she needed to figure out what to wear the next day. She shifted her focus to pictures of the women attending the function. Sheaths and sweaters, an occasional pantsuit. A picture of Nick's mom grinning over the success of the function. Her heart hurt for Amanda Kourakis.

But for Nick, too. He'd said his life would have been very different if his brother hadn't died. Now she saw how.

The next day, Nick arrived at the children's ward at one o'clock. His mother was already there, firing orders at the caterer and the three people sprucing up the ward's existing decorations. She had a photographer, of course. Her public relations firm would send a press release chronicling the event, complete with pictures. Kids would be kept in their rooms so the food, cookies, decorations and brightly wrapped gifts would all be a surprise when they stepped into the activities room.

When he hugged his mom, she said, "You're here early."

"I got antsy."

"Antsy?"

"Yeah. I was in my office, preoccupied with being here…" Picturing Leni in a new dress, trying to guess how she'd wear her hair, even though he knew that was wrong. "I was wondering how things were going and I figured I should just come down." So, he'd stop thinking about Leni and get his mind on the fundraiser.

"Well, I'm glad you're here!" She gave him another quick squeeze. "Why don't you walk around, take a look at things, make sure I'm not missing anything?"

He laughed. "You're not missing anything. You're too thorough. But I wouldn't mind sneaking a peek at what we have to eat."

He walked away, and his mom called, "You can look, but no picking! I want every tray to be perfect."

He glanced at the food and gifts, all beautifully displayed, and eventually found his way to the office of the director. She gave him a rundown of things that had happened in the ward in the past few months, purchases and the ward's wish list, which he tucked into his pocket as something to discuss with Leni. She had the kind of money that would allow her to be a benefactor. Talking to her about potential donations, responsibilities she might want to pick up, would get their relationship back on track. He shouldn't have kissed her the night they'd shopped, mostly because the sweet kiss had rocked him as much as the sexy one had.

Still, it wasn't himself he was worried about. It was Leni. He hadn't wanted to give her the wrong impression. But the kiss was an easy, natural goodbye kiss. Nothing to get excited about. So today he'd be cool. And she'd be cool, and they'd be fine.

But when he noticed it was one-thirty, his gaze drifted to the elevator. When she finally stepped out at almost a quarter till two, his breath stalled. Not because he was relieved that she'd come, but because she looked amazing.

She wore black high-heel boots and a green dress that exaggerated her eye color, with a black wool coat draped over her arm. Her hair had been left down to curl along her back and swirl around her when she moved. A man in a sedate suit stood beside her, but Nick recognized him as one of Jace's employees. Someone he could dismiss.

He walked over and, unable to stop himself, caught both of her hands. "You are stunning."

Leni's heart stuttered. She told it to stop, but how could she be neutral when he looked at her like that?

She laughed. "This is what a little money can do."

He laughed and addressed Chuck, the driver

Jace had assigned to her. "I think we're good here."

Leni frowned. "Good?"

"Sure. Everybody here is in the same tax bracket. Jace has security at all the entrances and exits." He smiled at Chuck. "No sense in overkill."

Chuck stepped into the elevator and Leni faced Nick. "So, what's going to happen here?"

"First, my mom will give a little speech about the good work the hospital does, then kids sit on Santa's lap and get gifts. Then there's a light lunch."

Her heart warmed. This was exactly the kind of charity she was looking for to share her wealth, but businessman Nick seemed to be back. She'd thought they'd ditched him days ago. But here he was again.

She glanced around, searching to see if there was an obvious way to bring fun Nick back. But she remembered the picture of this event from six years ago. The shot of his laughing mom, smiling dad and handsome younger brother—with bad boy Nick, who even though he looked totally out of place, had been here supporting the children's wing.

Obviously, this charity, this event, had been a family thing. Now it seemed like only Nick and his mom were involved.

She would be kind, especially to businessman Nick. "Sounds good."

He motioned to the left and said, "Let me take your coat," as a man in a black suit approached them. Leni handed the coat to Nick and he handed it to the guy in the black suit.

Nick's mom walked over. She took Leni's hands, leaned in, kissed her cheeks and said, "Thank you for coming."

Leni's heart broke a bit. Knowing what she knew now about Amanda losing a child and how it had changed her family, her life, she could have hugged her forever. "It's my pleasure."

"My son told me you are now a client of the firm."

She had to give points to Nick for that one. Though he'd given his mother a good explanation for her presence in their lives, he hadn't told her Leni was a Hinton heir.

"Yes. It's official."

"Well, that's wonderful." Amanda peeked at her watch. "I've gotta run. It's time for my greeting. We have to start the program exactly at two o'clock or the thing will run too long and I'm sure everyone has dinner plans."

Leni smiled and nodded as Amanda bustled away. The short talk she gave was both heart-rending and upbeat. Leni applauded with everyone else.

Nick motioned for her to walk down the hall. "Let's go to the activity room and watch the kids open gifts."

Leni and Nick followed his mom and stopped beside Santa, who told the kids to form a line.

Leni's heart shattered. There were children in casts and on crutches. Kids with shaved heads. Little children in wheelchairs.

As if reading her mind, Nick leaned in and whispered, "Most of these kids will be home for Christmas."

"Really?"

"Yes. Medicine is so different now. We're seeing more and more kids recover and go on to lead normal lives."

"That's fabulous."

"And something your dad was a part of."

She laughed. "Why, Nick Kourakis, are you trying to get into my pocketbook?"

He grinned at her. "You didn't bring a pocketbook."

"Well, it looks like I should have."

He laughed merrily. Her heart perked up and she was having a little trouble controlling it. How could she not like him more and more with each passing minute? Seeing the picture of his family before his brother died, she realized how difficult it must be for him. Not just because he was mourning, but because it was clear his family had suffered the kind of loss from which some families don't recover.

How could she not long to see him as happy as he had been six years ago?

Santa arrived, and she stood with Nick, enjoying the kids as they hopped on Santa's lap and gave their Christmas lists.

The wishes of the kids ran the gamut of silly and normal to sentimental and wonderful. One little girl wanted her grandmother to get a washer, so she didn't have to go to the Laundromat. From the corner of her eye, Leni watched Nick type her name into his phone.

She smiled at him and he smiled at her. That rush of adrenaline that she'd felt the first time she'd seen him raced through her. After last night's kiss and today's easy conversations, she didn't even try to stop it. He was a great-looking guy, who clearly loved these kids and his mom. He was good at his job. And thoughtful enough to fly to Kansas to help her and her mom through the worst day of their lives—even as he was clearly still struggling with his own loss.

There was no way in hell she could stop herself from falling in love with this man. If the situation ended with him not feeling the same way about her, she was going to end up with the biggest broken heart in recorded history. But today she just couldn't stop herself from letting go and letting herself feel everything her heart wanted to feel for him.

CHAPTER THIRTEEN

NICK SAW IT. She'd given him *that* smile, and he'd felt the same thing he'd felt the first time he saw her. Smitten.

He reminded himself that he didn't deserve her. But that didn't mean he couldn't fall for her. How could he not when she was light and simple, easy to be with? And real. So wonderfully real in a world that was filled with money and power and posturing.

Still, he'd have to be careful. He might long for the feelings she inspired in him. Might even want to indulge them if only in his own heart. But he couldn't really act on them.

So, he let her limo take her home and resisted the urge to call her that night. The next morning, despite the snow, he made it to the meeting Danny had set up for him to explain details of Mark Hinton's estate to her. Show her slides of houses, give her lists of companies and things like yachts and Jet Skis.

He hadn't expected he'd be needed this soon,

but Danny had explained that Leni was smart and adjusting to everything quickly. The more information they could get out of the way before they found the next heir, the better.

She wore a pink sweater and jeans with boots made for snow and he smiled to himself about her practicality. Something he didn't see a lot of in his world.

When Danny suggested lunch, he bowed out, blaming work and got into the elevator which returned him to the lobby. His phone rang before he could get outside, and he paused to take the call. As he stood talking to one of his managers, the elevator to Danny's office opened again and Leni walked out.

Alone.

He squeezed his eyes shut. He had no idea why she hadn't taken Danny up on is offer of lunch, but watching her walk through the lobby, out the revolving door into the hellacious winter storm, his heart stuttered. All the same, he told himself to give her time. She'd easily make friends. She'd easily fit in. She just needed time.

His chest tightened when he thought about how quickly and how easily she'd also find dates. With her looks and down-home charm, men would flock to her. He pulled in a breath to loosen his chest but went back to his call.

Watching her fall in love with someone else would be part of his penance.

* * *

Leni took her limo back to her hotel and busied herself searching real estate listings on the internet and trying to decide which of the three real estate agents Nick had recommended she'd choose to help her.

Eventually, she chose an agent and contacted her by email. Saturday morning, the agent called her and Sunday afternoon, they met at the coffee shop across the street from her hotel to talk about what she needed. Using her phone, the agent pulled up six potential condos and Leni chose three to see the following day. And the agent left.

Bored at three o'clock in the afternoon on a lazy Sunday, she nearly called Nick. But she hesitated. Friday, Saturday and now Sunday had gone by without a word from him except a very professional overview of her dad's holdings at Danny's office.

Did she really want to be the one to call?

She got a second latte, settled in on one of the stools at the counter and used her phone to research Mark Hinton again. Really curious about him now that she was hearing how he lived, how much he had and how alone he was. He could have had anything he wanted—except friends. Extrapolating from things Nick and Danny had said in their meeting, she realized he hadn't trusted anyone.

She scrolled through three of the websites dedicated to him, including one where people tried to guess his whereabouts. She shook her head with wonder. Didn't people have anything better to do?

"Hey."

She glanced up to see a youngish woman, maybe twenty-four, smiling at her. "Mind if I sit here?"

Leni shifted over a bit on her stool, as if she needed to make room for her, then told herself not to be silly. "Sure. I just need one chair," she added, making fun of herself for the way she'd shifted over to make room.

The young woman laughed and tucked a strand of her long black hair behind her ear. "I'm Sandy Wojack."

"I'm Leni." She stopped a bubble of panic that formed in her chest. If Mannington had a coffee shop, people would sit with other people all the time. If they hadn't been introduced, they'd introduce themselves.

But she was an heir of a multibillion-dollar estate. And in the thirteen days since Nick had found her in Mannington, nine of which she'd spent in New York City, no one had introduced themselves to her. No one had come up to her.

Of course, she hadn't been out much.

"I saw you with the real estate agent and was trying to overhear the addresses of the condos you were looking at."

Leni stiffened. Nobody in Mannington would admit to eavesdropping like that. "Oh."

"Real estate is so tight here, right?"

She had no idea. "Absolutely."

"I was hoping I could get a lead from your agent." She laughed. "But you're buying out of my price range."

And that felt downright weird. Nobody talked money with a stranger. At least, no one from Mannington did.

She reached to pick up her phone to gather her things and leave, and realized it was side-by-side with Sandy Wojack's phone. Not where she had put it…at least eighteen inches away from her.

Fear washed through her. Wasn't that how people cloned phones?

Hell if she knew!

"How did this get here?"

Sandy blinked innocently.

And Leni felt like an idiot. Sort of. She slid her phone into her expensive designer purse, lifted her even more expensive coat from the back of her stool and let her ridiculously expensive black boots carry her outside.

For the love of all that was holy, she might as well be wearing a sign that she had more money than she knew what to do with.

She raced back to the hotel, jumped inside her room and leaned against the closed door, her heart pounding. Not sure if she was panicking for nothing or if she'd just been identified, she sucked in a breath, raced to her hotel room phone and dialed Nick's number.

"I think I'm in trouble."

His voice hardened. "What kind of trouble?"

She told him the story of Sandy Wojack, and after he cursed, she burst into tears. "I don't know why I'm crying, except that it all felt really wrong, really odd." She took a breath. *"Invasive."*

"I'm coming over. Call Danny, tell him what you told me and then call room service and get us a really good bottle of scotch."

By the time Nick made it to her hotel room, she'd called Danny and had also taken a quick shower. The whole damned encounter had felt wrong and though the shower didn't ease her apprehensions, the warmth of it eased her nerves some.

Nick entered carrying Chinese food. "You're okay?"

"Yes. And I'm sorry. I feel really stupid for crying. Danny's not okay, though. He's going to look up cloning phones to see if she could have done that and he's calling his media contacts."

"He'll figure this out." He held up the bag of Chinese food. "Hungry?"

"Starving."

"Good. Is Danny calling back?"

"If he finds anything."

"Okay, we'll eat Chinese food, find a movie on pay-per-view and wait for his call."

Having him in the room made her feel safer somehow and that's when she began feeling foolish. Someone had sat down beside her at a coffee shop and started talking real estate. There was no sin in that. Yes, her phone had been moved and the girl—Sandy Wojack—had seen the condos she would be looking at—

Damn. Even trying to make it sound innocent, it was bad.

"I'm not going to be able to buy any of the condos I saw today."

"Not if we find out Sandy Wojack is a reporter." He winced. "Or that she sold your story to a reporter."

"Damn."

"You'll know to be more careful the next time."

"I will." She picked up the container of fried rice and slid some onto a paper plate provided by the Chinese restaurant. By the time she had a whole plate of wonderful-smelling goodies, Nick had the remote in his hands, searching for movies.

They watched a comedy for forty minutes, alternately eating and chatting, but as the reality of what had happened with Sandy Wojack sunk in, her stomach soured.

"I know this."

Nick peeked over. "You know what?"

"How much my dad had. And even how money makes people a little crazy."

"It's going to be fine."

"No. It's not." Just as her instincts told her she and Nick were falling in love, her instincts were telling her Sandy Wojack was a bad person. And her instincts were never wrong.

The chime of Leni's hotel room phone burst into the room and she and Nick exchanged a glance. He picked it up and said, "Hello?"

"It's Danny."

"It's Danny, Leni."

Leni let out her breath. "Put it on speaker."

Nick clicked the speaker button and said, "Hey, Danny, you're on speaker with me and Leni. What did you find out?"

"That Sandy Wojack's already tried to sell her story to three papers."

Leni squeezed her eyes shut.

Nick said, "How'd she figure it out?"

"She didn't. She was watching Leni because her clothes were expensive, and she was considering a seven-million-dollar condo. When the real estate agent left, she saw Leni reading about Mark Hinton on her phone." Danny took a breath. "She secretly took a few pictures of you before she sat down to talk to you. The woman must be a professional con artist or something because she told two of the papers she had the spyware to clone your phone."

Nick sat back on the red sofa. "Then she knows everybody involved and all of our phone numbers."

Leni shook her head and walked over to the wall of windows, looking out at Times Square.

Danny said, "Yes and no. Leni didn't text much. Her mom. A few friends. So, all Sandy really has is information about Leni's friends in Mannington and your number and my number. As well as the hotel number."

"Then she's not staying here tonight."

"No. She can't."

"She can stay with me."

For that Leni turned. "No."

She would not stay overnight with him. She wouldn't risk tumbling into bed because she was scared and helpless and overemotional. "There are hundreds of hotels in this city. Pick one."

Danny said, "How about if we pick one closer to my office, Leni?"

"That would be great."

"Call your real estate agent and cancel those showings tomorrow."

"Yes," Nick agreed. "I gave you three names. We'll move on to the next one."

Leni pulled in a breath. "Okay."

"Give me ten minutes," Danny said. "I'll have you in a hotel so secure even Nick will have to check in with your bodyguards."

"Okay."

CHAPTER FOURTEEN

THE UPROAR THE next day was beyond Nick's wildest dreams. He couldn't imagine what Leni was feeling. Her picture graced the front page of several newspapers, including national newspapers. The New York City television news programs showed the crowd of reporters outside the entrance to her Times Square hotel.

Danny had gotten her a new phone and when she called her mother with the new number, she'd had to explain that she'd been discovered and things were about to get weird. Hearing that, Nick had called Jace and Jace had dispatched two people to Kansas to protect her parents.

Nick watched it all with a huge hole in his heart for Leni. When noon hit, and her stomach growled, he got the strangest idea.

"What do you say we go out for dinner?"

She turned to him, her green eyes as big as two plates. "Are you kidding? Go out in that?"

She pointed at the window and he shrugged. "You can wear big sunglasses."

"In a restaurant?"

"You won't need them in the restaurant."

"Yeah, well, I thought I was safe in a coffee shop, too."

"You'll be safe. We'll go somewhere no one will know or care who you are."

"Mars?"

"Paris."

She gaped at him. "Paris?"

"Why not? It could be fun." He gave her a coaxing smile. "More fun than sitting in a hotel room."

He could tell from the look on her face that she couldn't argue that.

"Okay. Should I pack?"

"For an overnight trip."

She headed for the bedroom of her new suite where everything was shades of brown and gray with big blue throw pillows on the sofa and chairs.

While she dressed, Nick ordered sandwiches from room service, then he called his pilot. They ate lunch while the pilot prepped for the flight. Before they left, she asked for a few minutes in her bedroom. When she came out, she was wearing her old jacket, white turtleneck and jeans.

"That Sandy woman said she'd gotten curious about me because of how expensive my clothes were."

Her voice held a sadness that broke his heart.

She shrugged. "This outfit kept people away from me for a whole week. I like to wear it."

"Sure."

They rode down in the elevator and got into her limo. She barely said anything on the drive to the airstrip. When they stepped into the plane, Jace's two men followed them.

"This is weird."

Nick shrugged out of his parka. "Not really. Things will eventually calm down. Like your dad, you may find places to stay where no one cares who you are. Like Idaho."

Taking a seat, she laughed. "I don't think they'll care in Mannington."

"Really? No one will extort money or threaten your future kids?"

"I don't think so."

Sitting beside her, he smiled at her naivete.

"I like Mannington. I trust the people in Mannington, and I've been giving this whole money thing some thought. I've decided that since I can't live out my dream of being a social worker, I should find something to do to satisfy that need. At first when I was talking to Danny, I'd thought being on the boards of my dad's companies would work, but now I don't think that's a good idea. I don't want to be the face of a multibillion-dollar fortune."

"So?"

"I've decided to fix my town."

He chuckled. "How do you fix a town?"

"First, I'd invest in all the businesses. You

know, to kind of beef them up. Like new chairs and booths in the diner. A new oven for the bakery across the street because they're always complaining theirs is too small."

"Makes sense."

"Then I'd find a way to bring work to the town."

"Ah…so people don't have to move to Topeka to find work."

"Exactly. I don't think I'm trying to buy everybody's love because they already like me. But I do believe they will see that having me around will have its benefits."

He considered her idea—knowing that wouldn't even put a dent in the Hinton fortune—and finally said, "I like all your plans and I hope you won't be disappointed."

"I won't be."

He cut her a look. "You sound so sure."

"And you sound so cynical."

He laughed. "That's my old Leni."

"There is no old Leni or new Leni or nice Leni or sharp Leni. I am always going to be myself."

Relief whispered through him. Not because he was glad she would remain herself, but because she was back to being feisty. "That I believe."

"Good."

"Okay. Can I make a few suggestions for your plan?"

She gave him a confused look, but said, "Sure."

"Beef up your police department and fire companies."

Her face brightened as she thought that through. "That makes sense."

"Bring in a clinic. Staff it with enough doctors that it can be open at least sixteen hours a day."

"I like it. It means more jobs."

"True. But it's also a safety issue. You'll have a doctor available when you need one."

The reality of why she'd need that hit her and she sighed. "Yeah."

"Speaking of safety. How is your dad?"

"He's good. He and mom went online and looked up the doctors and hospitals his neurologist and I found for him. He has appointments with three neurosurgeons."

"Three?"

"The guy is looking at brain surgery. We want all the opinions we can get."

"Good idea."

They went back to discussing Mannington and Leni's ideas to make it cleaner, nicer, safer, with more jobs, but eventually her sleepless night took its toll and she drifted off. The peaceful expression on her face took his breath away. The longing to stay with her forever rippled through him.

But that was wrong. She deserved so much more.

Especially since she had a plan that made her feel safe. She hadn't said that was why she intended to spruce up her town, bring it life, but he knew that was at least part of it. She felt safe there, among people she knew. Still, if he accidentally let himself think of her being in his life, happiness filled him. The happiness of having her at his side, the male pride that she loved *him*. But he only let himself think like that for a second because it was wrong and when he remembered that, misery filled him.

He might not have been happy before he'd met her but at least he'd found purpose in growing the family business, living up to his dad's expectations. Now all that felt empty.

He didn't care. Empty. Not empty. It didn't matter. That was his life. All the life he deserved.

He called Marie who hustled to the front of the plane. He whispered, "Could you get us a blanket?"

She nodded and raced off, returning with a thick white wool blanket. He placed it over Leni, then yawned himself. It had been a long, miserable twenty-four hours. He reached over and took a section of the blanket to cover himself and within minutes was asleep.

Nick woke after three hours, but Leni didn't stir until they landed. Though it was seven o'clock at night in New York, it was two o'clock in the morning in France. And it was cold.

When the plane stopped completely, he signaled for Marie to take their blanket and bring their coats. "I'm sorry to tell you that it's a little chilly in France in December."

She blinked up at him. "I have my coat. It's not like we were planning on going to the beach."

"But we could. If you wanted to, we could simply tack a few days onto the trip and head for an island where it's warm enough to wear a bikini."

She chuckled. "Right. That's funny."

"No. That's your life now." But he saw what he was doing. Sadness and longing had him subtly trying to convince her to go somewhere they could be together. Somewhere her safety and his past wouldn't be an issue.

"And maybe that should be part of this trip. Maybe you should look around and realize you can go anywhere you want. Live anywhere you want."

She took a breath.

He told himself not to argue his case, but his mouth didn't listen. "I'm serious. You can be an island girl."

"I know. But I like my plan about Mannington."

He had to admit he did, too. And having her consider an island was just his stupid selfishness. He wanted her. He wanted to be with her, but not as himself. He wanted to hide or run and forget everything.

But that was even more wrong than trying to persuade Leni to give up her life, her friends, her parents for him.

She had responsibilities now.

He rose from his seat, took their coats from Marie and helped Leni into hers. They deplaned into the dead of night.

"I'm guessing there's a time difference."

He winced. "Yeah, I added the seven hours travel time to noon in New York and figured we'd get here for dinner. But in all the confusion I forgot the time difference."

She took a deep breath of the frosty air and glanced around as they walked to a waiting limo. "I see that."

"In a few hours we can have breakfast. Yummy pastry and rich dark coffee."

She laughed. "Sounds great."

He winced. "But then we have to get home."

"Really?"

"I also forgot the charity ball on Friday."

She gasped. "For the children's ward."

"Yes."

"Your mom wanted me to go to that."

"I'd like you to go to that."

The peace and quiet of the French countryside must have worked its magic because she smiled her Leni smile. "Then I'll go."

The drive from the airstrip was long but when they got close to Paris, Leni could see the lights of the Eiffel Tower and the trip suddenly felt real.

She was in *France*. She really could go anywhere she wanted. Do anything she wanted. As long as she could protect herself.

Because it was so late, Nick checked them into a gorgeous hotel. She expected them to go to separate rooms, but he opened the door on a suite.

"I know you're fine. I know you're safe," he said as they entered the room, bellman on their heels. "But I'll just feel better if you're within yelling distance."

Her mouth went dry. She knew he'd put a blanket over her while she was sleeping, then crawled under with her. The extreme circumstances they were battling were definitely bringing out his protective instincts...but what if they were bringing out more than that? Sharing a room... Would they be sharing a bed?

She thought back to their kiss and even though she knew they'd be an explosive combination, she didn't want to end up in bed because he was afraid. She wanted more kisses. She wanted him to woo her.

It was stupid to be such a romantic. But she was. She always had been and Nick was, too. He'd hinted at it right before he'd kissed her the first time in her mom's kitchen.

"Anyway," Nick said, glancing around the room that was soft shades of yellow with white sofas and chairs and bowls of white roses on every flat surface. "Those two doors are to the bedrooms. You can pick the one you want."

Disappointment and relief collided and flooded her. But disappointment won. He hadn't even thought of sleeping with her.

Which could be considered gallant.

Or prove that he didn't have the same feelings for her as she had for him—

Then why the blanket? Why share the blanket? She knew damned well there had to be more than one blanket on that plane.

She shook her head to clear it of the idiocy. She was tired. "It doesn't matter which room." She pointed to the one on the left. "I'll take that one. I still need some sleep."

"And when you wake up, I know the perfect café for breakfast."

She smiled and nodded, went into the room and face-planted onto the thick white comforter covering the big bed.

Soon she wouldn't have to worry about reporters or charlatans following her around. This situation itself was going to drive her crazy.

He made good on his promise of a café the next morning. Though it was cold, they sat outside drinking rich black coffee and eating pastries with names like cream puff, croissant, madeleine, macaron. With her wearing her old coat, they walked to the Eiffel Tower, along the Seine and then they had to go home.

But the trip had refreshed her. She'd put on new

jeans when she dressed that morning and one of her beautiful soft sweaters. But she'd also slid into her old jacket so that when they reached her New York City hotel and she got out of Nick's limo, she looked like an average tourist. Her bodyguards discreetly walked ten feet in front of her and at least ten behind. She didn't look at them. She didn't draw any attention to them or herself. She simply got into the elevator with the first one, climbed to the floor of her new hotel room and walked down the hall.

When she entered her room, the oddest sense filled her.

She hadn't been afraid in Paris and, damn it, she refused to be afraid now. This kind of sneaking around, pretending to be just an average person, walking into a hotel room while discreetly surrounded by bodyguards wasn't her.

She was stronger than this. Smarter than this. More easygoing than this. That's how she intended to behave from now on.

Nick checked on Leni over the next few days, but he didn't go to see her. He was already too tempted to do something that wasn't right, to change her mind about where she lived and how she lived. His selfishness was back and if he got too close, he'd want more and persuade her to give him more.

Because that's what he did best, persuade peo-

216 CINDERELLA'S BILLION-DOLLAR CHRISTMAS

ple to see things his way. The night his brother died he'd persuaded Joe to go out when he didn't want to. If he'd listened to Joe, his brother might still be alive now.

He couldn't forget that.

On Friday, he arrived at the ball early enough to ease his mother's fears about whether everything looked perfect. As opening time approached, he stood with his parents in an informal receiving line where they could welcome guests. He tried to tell himself he wasn't watching for Leni but when she appeared at the back of the line his heart stumbled.

Every time she walked into a room, she stole his breath, but tonight he wasn't sure he'd get it back. Her red gown clung to her breasts and tiny waist but belled out with layer after layer of soft, shiny red fabric. Her shoes must have had five-inch heels because she was taller than he'd ever seen her.

He laughed remembering the first time she'd worn high heels around him, thinking she was tall enough to kiss, and his heart twisted.

He'd never met anybody like her. Normal and fun, but tonight she looked like royalty. Her head high. Her smile real. Her face breathtaking.

As she inched her way toward him, he thanked his lucky stars that he'd already worked all this out in his head and wouldn't make a move on her. Then he realized something that stopped his heart.

This would be their last night together for weeks. Soon, she'd be leaving for Mannington for Christmas. She wouldn't return until she had to. He'd endure a quiet Christmas at his parents' where everybody thought about Joe but no one said a word. He'd feel it. He'd feel their anger and their loss. Then he'd go to work and avoid talking to anyone for weeks.

By the time she came back to New York, they'd both be so different they might not really like each other. Or, worse, their paths might only cross when Danny called them both into his office.

She finally reached his parents. His mother hugged her. His *father* hugged her. Probably because he now knew she was one of the three Hinton heirs.

Leni shifted away from his parents, and Nick held his breath. This was his last night with Leni as Leni. Their last night of being two people so attracted to each other they experienced an almost irresistible pull.

He didn't know how it would end, but suddenly he knew he couldn't let this opportunity pass.

Her eyes had been painted with green shadows that gave her a mystical air. Her hair was pulled up into something that looked like a ponytail of curls that cascaded to her shoulders. Her red dress sparkled as if someone had hidden glitter in the fabric that hugged her curves.

He took her hands. "You are stunning."

"Thanks. You don't look so bad yourself."

He glanced down at his tuxedo, then laughed. "I guess men are lucky. We don't have to figure out colors or styles. We just have to look good in black."

"Well, you are amazing in black."

Her heart could attest to that from the jump in her pulse when she saw him. Good God. Could a man be any sexier? From his height to his shiny hair to the way he held himself as if he'd been born in a tux.

He made being rich look really, really easy.

He caught her elbow and turned her toward the ballroom. "Why don't we get a glass of champagne?"

She motioned to the receiving line. "Don't you have duties?"

He shrugged. "I think I'm done."

Because he wanted to be with her? After days of a phone call or two to be sure she was okay, he wanted to be with her? Maybe just for one drink?

Probably. She wouldn't make a big deal of it. Wouldn't let her aching heart get too excited. He might look at her with longing in his eyes, but since Paris he'd treated her like a friend.

So, she smiled at him the way she would a friend. "I'd like a drink."

They walked into the room that had been filling with people. White poinsettias acted as centerpieces on tables covered in crisp white linen. But red and green accent lights added some whimsy, making the room festive. A string quartet played softly in a far corner.

Nick took two flutes of champagne from a passing waiter and handed one to her. "Merry Christmas."

She would have thought it odd that someone was wishing her Merry Christmas a week before the actual event. But that afternoon she'd been shopping for her parents, being told Merry Christmas by some very happy clerks.

They touched their glasses together with a soft clink and she took a sip of the most perfect champagne she'd ever tasted. She closed her eyes in ecstasy.

"So good."

He laughed. "I love that you close your eyes to savor."

And she loved that he used the word *love* because right now, in this moment, he wasn't looking at her like a friend. His gaze had softened and his smooth voice was velvety seduction.

Maybe he'd missed her? Maybe he'd decided to stop fighting?

He introduced her to a few friends and business

associates who were extremely curious about her but too polite to ask the questions she could see shimmering in their eyes. She made conversation about their jobs and families and everyone eagerly joined in. She might not have been born to money, but she did know people, how to be kind and polite. That was her and she'd already decided she wasn't losing herself.

As Nick swept her away from the last group, he laughed. "You're getting really good at this."

"I just decided to stay myself." She caught his gaze. "This is me. I'm not letting a bunch of crazy curiosity seekers ruin my life."

His head tilted as he studied her. "You're really okay?"

"I'm really okay."

"I knew you would be. I knew you'd figure it out."

For him, she would figure out anything. But she suspected in his own way, he probably knew that too, so she only smiled.

When it came time for dinner, he led her to his family's table where his father rose as Nick seated her.

Extremely glad for the online videos she'd found on etiquette, she took her seat, sending Nick a smile of thanks as he sat on the seat next to her.

She suddenly felt like Cinderella. Not at her first ball—the one where she'd lost her shoe. But the next ball. The one after the Prince had found her and told her he loved her. The one where he showed her off.

Because that's what this felt like. Nick had introduced her to friends and business associates and now she was dining with his parents, like part of their circle. It was heady fun, but there was a deeper message. She fit. And he liked that she fit. He liked *her* and he was done fighting it.

After dinner, they listened to a few speeches of thanks to volunteers and benefactors of the children's ward of the hospital, then the band began to play. She and Nick danced to the first few songs. Then his friends began asking her to dance. Nick would let her dance with three friends, then he'd rescue her, and they'd dance again.

She swore she really was Cinderella.

The night passed in a blur of champagne and laughter. Giggling on their way to the street and their limos, Nick stopped them in front of hers.

"This was so great. You made a usually dull event tons of fun."

And champagne had made *her* tipsy enough that she flattened her hands against his chest, feeling the smooth silk of his white shirt.

She looked up into his shiny dark eyes. "I think we're a good team."

"I think we are, too. So, I was thinking maybe we'd both take your limo." He caught her gaze.

"Say yes, because I already told my driver to go home."

Her chest tightened and breathing became difficult, the way it had the first time he kissed her. She knew this was it. He wasn't just going to kiss her again. He was coming home with her.

She worked not to sound nervous when she said, "Sure."

The driver opened her limo door and they slid inside. The door closed, cocooning them in a dark, silent world.

The limo pulled into traffic, but neither one of them said anything. Glad for the short trip, she stemmed her nervousness as Nick helped her out of the limo and led her to her suite.

The second the door closed behind them, he pulled her to face him. His head descended slowly, and she held his gaze, keeping her eyes open until the very last second. She wanted to see everything, every emotion that flickered in his dark, dark orbs. She wanted to remember everything on the night of the first time they'd make love.

CHAPTER FIFTEEN

EVERYTHING SUDDENLY FELT right in Nick's world. As he brushed his lips across Leni's, the sense of rightness morphed into pure pleasure. She tasted like champagne and happiness. Everything he wanted in this minute. Everything he needed to remember her by.

Because he would not sleep with her. It didn't matter that their luxurious kiss rolled through him like thunder or that his heartbeat pounded in anticipation of touching her. He would only take this so far.

He unbuttoned the silk jacket that matched her gown, knowing only thin fabric would separate his palm from her skin, but reminding himself that had to be enough. He wouldn't hurt her. He wouldn't edge his way into her world. He only wanted this taste.

So, he kissed her, her mouth eager beneath his desperate one. There was something hot and mysterious between them. There had been from the first second their eyes locked. Tonight, it rose like thick smoke from a raging fire.

A voice deep inside him told him this was it. Real love that offered peace and contentment. Maybe even a second chance. And he should grab it.

Another voice, the stronger voice, reminded him he didn't deserve it, but more than that *she* deserved better.

Still, he smoothed his hand along the silk of her bodice, knowing taut skin lie beneath. Temptation spiked, but his conscience tweaked again. He ached for this and he knew why. He wasn't looking for redemption that wasn't his to find. But a new start suddenly loomed on the horizon because everything about her was fresh and original. Unique. Wonderful. She would make his life an open door. He'd never want anyone else. Anything else.

But that was the point. He couldn't walk away from his life. He had commitments. Sins that couldn't be forgiven. A life that would drag her down.

Only a true sinner would drag someone like her into his private hell.

He pulled away from her. "I think I'd better get going."

Her gaze connected with his. "Why not stay?"

Her voice was soft, innocent. His walls yearned to crumble. Need tore through him.

Which was why he stepped back. He wouldn't hurt her, but he couldn't tell her that because he didn't want to get into a debate about his reasoning. He wasn't sure he'd win. So, he fudged a bit.

"It's late. I had a long day."

She walked her fingers up the buttons of his shirt. "I wouldn't make you do all the work."

He couldn't help it. He laughed. But he wouldn't let himself forget who he was and why he had to let her go.

He brushed a light kiss across her lips. "You're nuts."

"But I think that's why you like me."

He turned toward the door of her suite. "Yeah. You're probably right." He kept it light, simple, so she wouldn't spend the night wondering what she'd done wrong. But in that second, he vowed he would never see her again unless it was in his office or Danny's.

Leni woke the next morning dreamy happy. She yawned and stretched and could have stayed in bed all day, except she wanted to see Nick. It was Saturday, but that didn't guarantee he wasn't working.

The night before had been perfect. Though Nick had laughed when she'd said he liked her because she was a little crazy, she knew that was true. She'd sensed all along that he needed more happiness—maybe more craziness—in his life. Now he saw it, too.

The most amazing idea hit her. She threw back the covers, climbed out of bed, ordered coffee and toast from room service, then called the concierge.

"I need to find a small Christmas tree and decorations."

He told her she could order a tree and have it delivered, then directed her to two nearby places where she could get sparkly ornaments, some tinsel and lights. He again suggested she could have them delivered too but she wanted to be the one delivering them.

After a quick shower, she called Jace and asked him for Nick's address. When he asked why, she told him about the Christmas tree and, though he hesitated, he told her the driver knew the address.

Two hours later, she had a small tree in her limo trunk, two bags of simple ornaments and happiness in her heart. She and her bodyguard walked into the lobby. The doorman's eyebrows rose.

"I guess I have to be buzzed up to Mr. Kourakis's condo."

His eyebrows rose even higher. "Mr. Kourakis?"

"Yes."

He hesitated a second, but said, "Let me call him."

He called, gave Leni's name and after a wince,

he hung up the phone. "He's on his way out for the day, but he'll see you."

That struck her oddly. Still, Nick had always been a difficult man. She knew he'd want to see her. He might not like surprises, but he did like kissing her and she liked kissing him. And whether he wanted to admit it, he needed a Christmas tree.

Nick waited by the elevator for Leni. When the door opened, she walked out holding two bags, with a bodyguard behind her carrying a three-foot Christmas tree. He nearly laughed.

But he couldn't. He'd given her the wrong impression the night before and now he had to fix it.

She set the bags down and slipped out of her coat. "I came here to spice up your condo, give you some Christmas cheer."

After instructing the bodyguard to set the tree, already in a small tree stand, on the table by the window, he dismissed him.

When the elevator door closed behind him, Nick folded his arms across his chest. "How do you know I didn't already have a tree?"

She laughed, rose to her tiptoes and brushed a quick kiss across his lips. "Lucky guess."

Something soft and warm floated through him when she kissed him. He longed to grab and savor it, but he couldn't. Leaving her the night before had been the hardest thing he'd ever done and now he'd have to say goodbye again.

Except this time, she had to understand this was the end of anything romantic between them.

She took the two bags of ornaments to the table, removed the boxes and put a bright red ball on one of the tiny limbs.

"Look, Leni. I think you and I have to talk."

"Talk while I decorate. Any chance you have coffee?"

"I can make you a cup, but... Listen." He nearly lost the struggle inside him. She looked so perfect in his home. And one by one, as the brightly colored balls filled the small tree, the spirit of Christmas, the memories of happier days and what the week before Christmas was supposed to feel like, filled him.

He reminded himself that he didn't want to hurt her, walked over, took the ornament from her hand and led her to the sofa.

She sat, but he didn't sit beside her. He lowered himself to the chair across from her, put his elbows on his knees and took a breath. He was going to have to tell her the truth. He didn't know why he hadn't realized that all along, but he saw it now.

"I'm not the nice guy you think I am."

"Yes, you are."

"No. See? That's what's wrong here. You have this vision of me being a nice guy that's not true.

If I take what you're offering, I'm going to hurt you."

"I don't think so."

He leaned forward a bit more. "You know my brother died. What you don't know is that he died because of me. My father is angry. After five years, my mother is still confused about how we're supposed to go on without him. But we all know it's my fault he died. I all but dragged him out in an ice storm. I was home from my gallivanting and wanted to have some fun."

He pulled in a harsh breath, ran his hands down his face. "I see everything from that night in slow motion in my head. Him trying to talk sense into me. Me telling him I was a Navy SEAL. I'd done things that would amaze him. I could certainly drive in a little ice. My parents angry because they didn't want us to go out. But I kept insisting and, in the end, I won. The roads were worse than anything I'd ever seen. But I got it in my head that this was like a mission and I needed to do it."

Memories of that night froze his chest, filled him with self-loathing.

"The few cars on the road were slipping and sliding but I was okay. Then I lost control and I couldn't even tell you how many cars I hit or how many hit me. I banged my head and blacked out and when I came to, paramedics were shouting about Joe. I looked over and he was so still. So quiet."

He stopped. He couldn't level his breathing, as those minutes came back full force. Paramedics scrambling. Firemen shouting. The fear that his brother was dead racing through him like a wildfire.

"You think you killed your brother?"

"I know I killed my brother. The accident might not have been my fault but going out was. Both of my parents warned me. Joe argued. My dad got mad." He shrugged. "I wouldn't listen. Now I have parents who look at me and see the guy who killed their son. It's all I can do to handle the burden of that.

"Losing my brother drained something from my soul. My family is never going to get over this because we can't blame fate. We can't come to terms with it because, when we try, all we have is the fact that I pushed when I shouldn't have. You're a good person. Too good for that kind of life. Too good for me."

"Nick…"

He rose from his chair. "No. Don't you get it? It's been five years and we can't move on. You do not know what it's like to look at your parents and realize you took away their good son. The son who stepped up to run the family business, when I refused to settle down and globe-trotted like the world owed me fun. He's the one who bought the best Christmas gifts and took Mom and Dad to brunch once a month. You don't know what it's like to have to try to be everything my brother would have been to make up for cockiness, arrogance." He shook his head and fell to his seat again. "You don't know what it's like to come home at night with that day's pressure morphing into the next day's stress, sprinkled with guilt and the grief of *my* loss. While everyone feels sorry for my parents. No one remembers I lost a brother, too."

"Oh, Nick…"

She rose and knelt in front of him, but he gently nudged her back, so he could stand, then help her stand.

"I won't drag you into that. But more than that, I know I don't have the mental energy to be the kind of man you deserve."

Leni nodded, the whole story swirling around in her head as she desperately worked to understand him. All along she'd known something was wrong. All along she'd known it somehow connected to his brother. But she'd never taken in the signs. She'd ploughed ahead, believing that something as strong as what stirred between them would conquer anything.

But she heard the pained resignation in his voice. He'd killed his brother. He was bruised and broken. And he was correct. That was the kind of emotional wound a family only got over with courage and work.

He'd been telling her that all along, pushing away all along and she hadn't listened.

She was an idiot.

No, she was the seven-year-old foster child, desperate for parents to love her, who always wished and hoped and saw things that weren't there because she so desperately wanted love. Wanted everyone to be happy. Wanted the world to work the way it should.

And she'd always ended up hurt. First, her dad didn't step up to help her sick mom. Then her mom dropped her off and never looked back. Three families had her as a foster kid and all three asked for her to be moved on to another home.

Not only did she know what it was like to be the star in a drama that was totally out of her control, she knew there were some things that didn't work out. Just as there were some wounds an outsider couldn't heal.

She slid her coat from the back of a chair, where Nick had laid it, but glanced back at the tree. She'd had such good intentions and worried that leaving it behind would only bring back bad memories for him, but in the end she decided to leave it.

Maybe it was time he faced some things. Maybe the tree would push him to do that?

Maybe then he'd realize they should be together...

In her head, she cursed herself for her wishful thinking. She was always like this. Hopeful. Positive. But the world wasn't always a positive place and not all answers were easy. She knew that. She had a mom who had abandoned her. A father who hadn't wanted her at all. She'd been *lucky* the Longs had found her.

Not everybody was so lucky. Not everybody's life worked out.

And she had no right to interfere. Despite her education and her longing to help him, she couldn't.

Horrible sadness rose in her. A combination of the grief she felt rolling from him in waves and her own grief for him.

As the elevator door closed behind her, sorrow for Nick rose in her. He should be the happiest guy on the face of the earth. Instead, he might actually be the most broken.

Tired, worn down, angry with herself for pushing Nick, Leni removed her coat in her suite, called Jace and told him she wanted to go home. Back to Mannington.

She almost called her mom to pick her up at the private airstrip, but she decided to rent a car instead. Her brand-new bank card was like a little miracle worker. She never had to ask the price of anything. She gave the card number to the clerk on the phone and she got anything she wanted.

Tonight, she wanted an SUV delivered to the airstrip to get her through the Kansas snow and home.

Home.

That's where she needed to be. That's where she was who she was supposed to be. Not some New York socialite who got herself involved in things that were over her head, things she couldn't fix. Kansas was where she belonged.

Evening arrived as she drove the hour to her parents' house. She pulled the big SUV into the driveway, grabbed one of the three suitcases with her new clothes in them and headed inside.

Opening the door, she called, "I'm home!"

Wearing an apron, her mom peeked out of the kitchen. "Leni! What are you doing here? We thought you weren't coming until Christmas Eve."

Not about to tell her mom she'd fallen in love with Nick and forced him to relive the worst night of his life as he told her he didn't want what she wanted, she fibbed just a little bit.

"I was sitting in my room and I thought, 'I should be making cookies right now,' and here I am."

"Because you want to bake cookies?"

"Because I do whatever I want now."

Her dad came up behind her mom. "Don't let that go to your head, Kitten."

Oh, she wouldn't. She'd learned her lesson with

Nick Kourakis. He'd given her every sign, every hint, that his family was in real emotional trouble and she'd missed it.

She thought of Nick casually mentioning his brother when they were skating but not being able to elaborate and her eyes drifted shut. He'd been so wonderful. Every time she'd had a problem like her dad's hospitalization or when Sandy Wojack told the world she was an heir, he'd been there.

She'd genuinely believed he loved her because everything he did for her was so natural, so honest, as if it had come right from his heart.

But he was the one who'd been in real pain and though she'd seen it she hadn't realized the depth of it and she'd pushed him.

Remorse shivered through her, hurting her to her core.

She took a breath. Reminded herself that she couldn't do anything about what had happened between them and that she'd be careful from here on out, wouldn't barge ahead, would pay closer attention to people, the way she'd been taught at university.

She shrugged out of the big parka she'd bought on her spending spree and hung it on a hook by the door, then rubbed her hands together. If it killed her, she would be happy. She would not let her parents see how upset she was.

"So? What are we making?"

"The cutout cookies that you like so much."

The same cookies she'd given Nick the weekend her dad had been in the hospital.

She fought the urge to weep. He'd always been there when she needed him, and she'd missed the signs that he needed her more.

"We'll ice them," her dad said proudly. "Then decorate. Maybe with sprinkles."

Her dad's happiness being able to do such a simple thing like make cutout cookies made her laugh. She breathed again. Told herself this was where she needed to be until she sorted out everything in her head. But what was there to sort? Money hadn't bought Nick's family happiness. Her love hadn't healed Nick. Her pushing had hurt him.

Her mom made two big bowls of batter which they refrigerated while she and her dad played a quick game of Yahtzee. When the dough had chilled, she reached for the first bowl of batter.

"Oh, sweetie, get an apron." Her mom motioned toward Leni's pink cashmere sweater. "You don't want to ruin that."

"Why? I can always buy another." The words came out choppy, mixed with tears and confusion.

Having money was such an odd thing. So much good, but so much bad.

"Kitten?"

The tears spilled over. "I found out some things

today that broke my heart. Especially since I made things worse."

Her dad put his arm around her. "What? What happened?"

"Nick and I seemed to be getting involved romantically." She sniffed. "He always pulled back and I decided to push, and he told me that his brother died in an accident and he'd been driving and he's not over it. Neither are his parents. But I pushed, and he had to tell me, and I knew I'd done nothing but bring back bad memories."

Her parents exchanged a glance. Her mom said, "You didn't know."

"I realize that." She rubbed her hands down her face. "But I keep getting these odd, disjointed memories of us having fun and being happy and I feel like I missed something. Like there was something I should have done."

"Oh, honey." Her mom sat her down at one of the kitchen stools. "You always wanted to change the world. But there are things you can't fix."

"Not even with money," her dad quietly said. "But that doesn't mean you stop trying."

Her dad's words comforted her. Especially when she remembered her plans for Mannington. Jobs. Money for the diner, grocery store and bakery. A bigger police force. A clinic.

Calm flitted through her and took root. Keeping busy was exactly what she needed to do.

That and stay away from Nick. She'd really

thought that whatever hummed between them was good. But all it seemed to do was remind him of what he couldn't have.

Her heart broke for him, but it broke for herself, too. She loved him and she'd hurt him.

Nick left the half-decorated tree exactly as it was on his dining room table. Every morning it mocked him. Every night it made him wish he could just walk over and hang the rest of the ornaments like a normal person.

By Wednesday, he couldn't go to work.

Thursday, he couldn't get out of bed.

Friday, he got up, made coffee and stared out the window at Central Park. None of the tricks he used to force himself back to life after his brother died were working. He was hungry. He was tired. But he was too broken to care.

The sound of his elevator doors opening turned him from the window. "Dad?"

"I heard you weren't at work."

Oh, God. Just what he didn't need: a lecture from his father. "I think I had a touch of the flu." Leni asking him if he lied to his parents a lot popped into his head and he didn't know whether to laugh or cry. He *missed* her. He felt that more than the grief and remorse over losing his brother, and then that brought new pain. New self-loathing. He had no right not to miss his brother. To push him aside. To forget him.

His dad strolled into the living area. "Your mother was sort of hoping you were holed up with that Long girl."

The preposterousness of his dad's statement made him hiss out a breath. "What?"

"You like her."

He did. So much. Too much. He walked from the window to the sofa. His sweatpants baggy after days of not eating. "What difference does it make?"

"It makes a lot of difference." His dad sat on the sofa. "You mother thought Leni was helping you get beyond some of your grief."

"I'll never get beyond this."

His dad's face grew solemn, so sad Nick couldn't remember ever seeing that expression before. "You have to get beyond this."

Nick sat on the chair he'd sat on to tell Leni to leave. To explain why he couldn't love her. He tried to say something but nothing came out.

"You liked Leni, right?"

He groaned internally at having this conversation with the father who pushed him and yelled at him, but he was dutiful now. So, he didn't argue.

"Of course, I did."

"Your mother thinks she was nature's way of nudging you to finally get beyond all this."

He sniffed. "My mother thinks a lot."

"Yeah, well, I took the job in the beginning. I forced you to work. I pushed you and yelled at you and made you get up every day and go to the office and have a purpose."

Nick stilled. "You didn't boss me around because you were angry with me?"

"No! I didn't want you to sink into a depression so far we'd lose you. Do you think I wanted to force you to work? I knew how hard Joe's death was on you. I *knew* you blamed yourself. Suffered in silence. And I knew if we let you go on like that, you'd never recover."

Thinking back on those days, seeing them in a new light, brought tears to his eyes. Everything was so confused. "I'm not exactly recovered now."

"Actually, son, I think that's what's nagging at you. You *are* recovering. You want to move on. But part of you won't let you. Holding onto the guilt is your penance."

Nick took a breath. "Oh, yeah?"

"Your mom and I went to therapy. Not for us. To figure out how to help you. That was our therapist's conclusion. Your guilt is how you think you make amends. But all you're doing is losing your life, too. Your mom and I don't want to lose both of our sons. Now that we finally see this light of hope, we're not letting it pass." His dad rose. "I won't push. Neither will your mom. This has to be up to you. But you like her. Maybe even love her. And it's time. We miss Joe, but we miss you, too." He paused, put a hand on Nick's shoulder. "We want you back. The real you."

The real him? The happy-go-lucky guy who only wanted fun was gone.

And though his dad might think he wanted the old Nick back, Nick wasn't that guy anymore.

He didn't want to be. He liked who he was now.

Leni would tell him that was vain.

He laughed. Then sniffed as the elevator doors closed on his dad. Setting aside his grief was too much. Too, too much.

He thought of skating with Leni. He remembered how he'd thought of Joe in a good way and how he'd been able to think about him without dwelling on it.

He thought of the Irish pub, telling her about his real self and having her nestle against him as they walked back to her hotel.

He thought about kissing her, being drawn in, always thinking about a future with her because that's what he'd been fighting. The knowledge that he wanted more with her.

He'd sent her off in the worst possible time of year in the worst possible way. He'd ruined her Christmas with his bluntness.

But he also might have ruined his one chance with her. She was a smart woman. He'd told her to move on and she'd probably listened.

He rubbed his hands down his face. His horrible life collided with the possibility of a new one. Strength he never realized he had punched its way up from his soul.

He missed Leni with an ache that gave spark and breath to the new yearnings struggling for life. His life.

His dad was right. He had to move on.

But could he?

And if he did, would Leni even want him anymore?

It took far too long for Nick to get from New York to Mannington. And when he got there, he froze. The Long house was dark. Still, he knocked. But no one answered.

It flitted through his mind that her dad might have had a seizure, but their network was too strong. She'd have called Danny and Danny would have called him.

So maybe they were at Christmas Eve services?

Suddenly a light came on in what Nick knew to be the kitchen, so he knocked again.

With her parents on their way to bed, Leni finished the last chapter of her book and almost turned out her light but there was a knock at her door.

Emotionally and physically exhausted, she walked to the kitchen to turn on the light, then into the living room where she opened door to find Nick.

Her chest tightened and hope rose, but she reminded herself of everything he'd told her. She'd pushed him into admitting the worst secret anyone could have and he'd explained that was why he didn't want a relationship.

She'd done enough damage to this man. She wouldn't do anymore. So, she smiled politely and said, "What are you doing here? Did something happen with the estate?"

"No. I'm visiting you."

Her heart hurt just looking at him. His eyes were tired as if he hadn't slept in days. His chin and cheeks had at least three days' growth of beard. Now that she knew the extent of his grief, his pain, everything inside her hurt for him.

"Can I come in?"

"Sure. I'm sorry! I should have let you in right away." She wouldn't be so foolish as to believe he'd come here because he loved her. The things he'd told her were too deep to be dismissed in a few days. But maybe he'd come to talk. They'd always been able to talk. And maybe she *could* help him?

He stepped inside and shrugged out of his parka, which she hung on a hook by the door. "I missed you."

That broke her heart. She wanted it to mean a thousand different things, but knew it was merely proof she'd insinuated herself into his life. "I missed you, too."

She motioned for him to sit on the chair and she sat on the sofa across from him.

"I had a long talk with my dad. My parents would like me to fall in love with you."

She would have laughed at the second part of his confession, but the first part threw her. "You had a long talk with your dad?"

"He told me he'd pushed me after Joe died because he knew my grief and guilt were too much to handle. That if he hadn't given me a purpose with running the family business, I might not have ever recovered."

She pictured his gruff dad saying that, then realized she might have interpreted his dad all wrong. What she saw as gruffness might have been his desperate way of keeping Nick from crumbling.

"He's probably right."

Nick leaned forward, his elbows on his knees, his hands clasped. "They've watched me take the blame for Joe these past five years, wondering if I'd ever get beyond it."

"Oh." How sad for them. How sad for Nick.

"Then you came into the picture and they said I changed."

"You had." She'd seen him changing, loved that he could be so fun with her.

"Their thought is that you nudged me back into the real world because I really liked you."

Her heart stuttered. "What do you think?"

He met her gaze. "That they were right."

"So, all the pushing I did wasn't bad?"

"You didn't push."

"I wasn't the desperate foster kid once again looking for love?"

"First of all, you have love. Your parents adore you. But, second, we were drawn together. From the second our eyes met the first time, I felt it. You are the perfect woman for me. You make me laugh. You make me think. You got me out of my condo more than I'd been out in five years. And you pick good Christmas gifts. My mother loved that kimono thing. We did our Christmas this afternoon, so I could come here to see you."

A small laugh escaped. She didn't see the grief and pain that had been on his face the day he'd told her about his brother. Everything felt washed clean.

He sat back, ran his hands down his face. "I hope I didn't ruin what we had. My life was a mess. But I'm ready to move on. Though I'll never forget what happened, never forget Joe, he wouldn't want me to live the way I have been."

"From the things you'd said, he sounded like a good brother."

He shook his head. "He was."

They were quiet for a minute. Leni took a

breath. She felt a nudge. An odd sensation that someone was telling her it was her move. That he'd dwelled enough on the past and she was the one helping him move into the future. "Want a cookie?"

He laughed. "The iced ones?"

"Made them myself with my dad and mom."

She led him into the kitchen. Pulled milk from the refrigerator and a container of cookies from the cupboard. Before she could open either, Nick caught her by the waist and spun her around.

He pressed his lips to hers, kissing her long and deep and she melted into him.

When he finally broke the kiss, he said, "I think I love you."

She slapped his arm playfully. "You goof. I know I love you."

"Even though you have more money than me now?"

She pretended to ponder that. "We'll see how it goes." Then she bounced to her tiptoes and kissed him this time.

"You know I expect you to woo me."

"Does anybody really woo anybody anymore?"

"I don't know. I don't care. But I want wine and roses, to be taken to dinner…"

"And trips to France?"

Her eyes widened. "Yes! More trips to France."

He kissed her again, not desperately, as he had before, but with a simple longing that matched the beating of her own heart, the buildup of hope that she wouldn't be alone anymore.

They really were a good pair. The best pair. Because they both understood that life wasn't always easy, but they could handle it.

Together.

As USUAL ON Christmas Eve night, snow fell on Mannington, Kansas. One year after their first Christmas together, Nick and Leni left the totally remodeled Family Diner, which they now owned and which they paid George handsomely to manage. The old Christmas bells that typically hung from the streetlights had been cleaned up and repainted. Red ribbons graced the parking meters. The storefronts for the bakery, coffee shop, auto mechanic and grocery had been renovated. All the sidewalks had been repaved.

Wearing a black leather jacket and to-die-for black boots with jeans and a new white turtleneck sweater, Leni took a long drink of air. "Do you think your mom will like what we got her for Christmas?"

"I'm not exactly sure how you had time to shop when you were arranging to move one of Hinton Industries' manufacturing plants here."

"I had a little help from a special Santa."

Nick laughed. "I'm glad you figured out how

to get help." He glanced at her. "It's been a busy year for you."

"And you."

"Yeah, but I didn't become wealthy overnight, meet a new brother and sister, go through a complicated surgery with my adoptive dad and singlehandedly become the redevelopment authority for one very happy small town."

She grinned. Becoming a Hinton heir had been one surprise after another. Fixing up her small town, making it somewhere everybody loved to live, had been the obvious thing to do. But finding real love with Nick, finding a partner, had made it all like a great adventure.

"It was a fabulous year."

As always when she said the word *fabulous*, they exchanged a glance and laughed.

"Now, you have to plan a wedding."

She took in a deep drink of air. "Is this a proposal?"

"Yes." He laughed. "Finally." He pulled a ring box from his jacket pocket, paused in the street and got down on one knee. "Leni Long, will you do me the honor of being my wife, my life partner, person destined to spend most of our money?"

Though she had been expecting the proposal, tears filled her eyes. "Yes."

He got up and kissed her. As always, her heart warmed, then her limbs warmed, then heat filled her. Somedays she couldn't believe this man loved her. Other days, she couldn't believe she'd managed so many years without him.

They broke the kiss and smiled at each other. Looking at her beautiful ring, she said, "Where should we get married?"

"Well, your dad loves the Key West house."

She pondered that, gazing around at the new storefronts as they walked through the snow on their way to the house they'd built as their home base. His New York penthouse was empty more than it was occupied these days.

Friends said hello and waved as they walked by. Snow sparkled in the glow of the streetlights. The sound of the choir rippled out from the well-lit church where Christmas Eve services were being held.

This was and always would be her home.

She stopped Nick. "I think I'd like to get married here."

He glanced around. "Here?"

"On Christmas Eve."

"Christmas Eve?"

"And I'd like to invite the whole town."

He gaped at her. "That's fifteen *hundred* people."

"I know!" She laughed merrily. "But we can afford it."

He shook his head, but when he looked around, he saw what she saw. Not merely a group of houses and businesses, but friends who sometimes felt like family. He saw hope. He saw the future.

He slid his arm across Leni's shoulders and began walking again. "I suppose you're going to want to build a hall big enough for fifteen hundred people to celebrate."

"And maybe expand the church."

He threw his head back and laughed. The minute Leni had entered his world, he'd gotten his life back.

As for his love of adventure? He had more than a feeling this woman was about to take him on the ride of his life.

* * * * *

Look out for the next story in
The Missing Manhattan Heirs trilogy
Coming soon!

And if you enjoyed this story,
check out these other great reads
from Susan Meier

Falling for the Pregnant Heiress
A Diamond for the Single Mom
Carrying the Billionaire's Baby
The Spanish Millionaire's Runaway Bride

All available now!